"I want you so badly, Noah, I ache."

Natalie nipped lightly at his jaw, then used her tongue to soothe the love bite. "Stop treating me like a fragile piece of glass," she continued. "I swear I won't break."

Bracing his hands on either side of her hips on the desk to keep from touching her, Noah shuddered, holding fast to his dwindling resolve. "Natalie—"

"Don't tell me no," she whispered as her lips traveled up to his ear. "I need the closeness of making love. I might have lost parts of my memory, but not my desire for you."

Noah squeezed his eyes shut, battling between right and wrong.

Taking his silence as acquiescence, Natalie pulled his shirt from the waistband of his jeans, shoved it up and over his head, then tossed it to the floor. She flattened her palms on his bare chest, caressing his flesh. Then her breathing deepened as she let her fingers drop lower.

"I want you, Noah," she said huskily, lifting one leg along his thigh so she could rub herself against his erection. "Touch me, and you'll see for yourself."

A man could take only so much. And that moment, Noah knew he wouldn't be able to refuse her this time....

Dear Reader,

You've met Noah Sommers in my two previous "Seduction" books, and I'm thrilled to finally be able to give him his own story in *The Ultimate Seduction*. The title of this book pretty much sums up Noah's downfall as he finds himself protecting Natalie Hastings, the woman he's desired for months. Their relationship is not only sudden and unexpected, but also wildly erotic. It's a good thing there's a supersexy line like Blaze, because this story delivers forbidden pleasures and red-hot sexual tension! It will leave you breathless.

I hope you enjoy Noah and Natalie's sexy, *seductive* story. Be sure to check my Web site at www.janelledenison.com for updated information on many more Blaze and Temptation novels to come. I always love to hear from my readers. You can write me at P.O. Box 1102, Rialto, CA 92377-1102 (send a SASE for goodies!) or at janelle@janelledenison.com.

Enjoy the heat!

Janelle Denison

Books by Janelle Denison

HARLEQUIN BLAZE

HARLEQUIN TEMPTATION

THE ULTIMATE
SEDUCTION

Janelle Denison

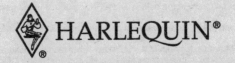

HARLEQUIN®

TORONTO • NEW YORK • LONDON
AMSTERDAM • PARIS • SYDNEY • HAMBURG
STOCKHOLM • ATHENS • TOKYO • MILAN • MADRID
PRAGUE • WARSAW • BUDAPEST • AUCKLAND

This book is dedicated to Kathy Boswell,
Suzanne Coleburn, Elizabeth Benway, Cindy Penn,
Yvonne Hering and all the other readers and reviewers out there
who work so tirelessly to promote the romance genre.
Thank you for your unending support.

And to Don, a champion of romance and my biggest fan.

ISBN 0-373-79065-1

THE ULTIMATE SEDUCTION

Copyright © 2002 by Janelle Denison.

This edition published by arrangement with Harlequin Books S.A.

® and TM are trademarks of the publisher. Trademarks indicated with
® are registered in the United States Patent and Trademark Office, the
Canadian Trade Marks Office and in other countries.

Visit us at www.eHarlequin.com

Printed in U.S.A.

1

"IF I HAD TO CHOOSE one guy in this place to get naked with, I'd pick Noah Sommers. He's so damn sexy." Gina fanned herself with a cocktail napkin and slanted Natalie Hastings an envious glance. "Unfortunately, there's only one woman in this bar he's interested in, and it certainly isn't *me*."

With a patient smile, Natalie set down her serving tray at the end of the mahogany-and-brass bar as Murphy poured drinks for the waitresses to deliver to the Saturday evening customers. Her friend's insinuation was as clear as the crystal hanging from the glass racks overhead. Noah Sommers wanted *her,* and for the past nine months he'd made his interest in her blatantly obvious, despite how many times she'd turned down his advances.

Unerringly, her gaze sought and found the man in question, a gorgeous male specimen with dark, tousled hair, striking blue eyes and a lean, honed body made for sin of the carnal variety. He'd certainly inspired a few private fantasies of her own.

He stood across the room in the gaming area of Murphy's Bar and Grill playing a round of pool with one of his good friends, Bobby Malone. As Noah lifted a bottle of beer to his lips, she admired the strong line of his jaw and the broad chest that filled out his plain blue T-shirt. Snug, faded jeans encased lean hips, muscular thighs and long, strong legs.

Oh, yeah, the man was sin incarnate.

Noah turned his head as Bobby made his shot and caught her looking his way. A slow, sexy grin eased up the corner of his mouth and he winked at her, causing a tingling warmth and awareness to pervade her entire body. Suppressing her sexual reaction as she'd taught herself to since her last relationship, she smiled back and returned her attention to her drink order.

"Don't you have anything to say for yourself?" Gina teased. "Or are you just playing hard to get with Noah?"

Natalie rolled her eyes at her friend. "You know I don't fraternize with the customers." A personal rule she'd established for herself, and one Noah sorely tempted her to break with his devastating smile and male charm.

"Or anyone else for that matter," Gina added as she loaded drinks onto her tray. "And Lord knows with that killer body of yours you could have just about any man you wanted."

Natalie inwardly cringed at Gina's assumption. If anything, she tried to downplay the centerfold curves that turned heads, but the bar uniform she was required to wear—jeans and a kelly-green T-shirt with "Murphy's Bar And Grill" emblazoned across her well-endowed chest—didn't hide much.

Reaching for a wedge of lime, Natalie settled the garnish on top of the bottle of Corona on Gina's tray. "Trust me, this body is more a curse than a blessing." Her lush figure had brought her more heartache than joy, more insecurities than confidence, not that she'd expect anyone to understand what she'd been through before coming to live in Oakland, California, nine months ago.

Gina glanced down at her own insubstantial chest, then back at Natalie, her brow raised with amusement. "Pardon me, but my triple A's tend to disagree."

Natalie shook her head as she refilled a bowl of shelled peanuts for Gina's customers, then her own. "You know how the saying goes…you always want what you don't have." The statement certainly held true for her. She'd spent too many years as a young girl wishing for a flat chest and a couple of pounds off her hips, not that anyone had granted her request.

"I'm very familiar with the saying," her friend said with a toss of her dark brown hair. "And I covet *those*." Her hazel-eyed gaze dipped briefly to Natalie's chest. "I'm hoping the 'be careful what you wish for' saying comes true for me."

Natalie laughed, and Gina sashayed off to deliver her drinks, garnering a fair share of male attention as she crossed the room. In Gina's case, the ogling and playful come-ons of the male patrons were appreciated. In Natalie's case, she tolerated the comments and stares as part of the job and the reality of her life.

At the age of twelve she'd been wearing a size 36B bra, along with acquiring curvaceous hips and long legs that had made her feel like a giraffe. Her bust size had eventually increased to a 36D, and by the time she'd graduated high school she'd learned that most boys and men looked at her and thought of one thing: sex. They'd dated her believing she'd put out, and were sorely disappointed when she didn't allow their wandering hands to make it inside her blouse or pants. Even the boy at the last foster home she'd lived at until the age of eighteen had attempted to coax her into his bed, to no avail.

Amazingly, she'd remained a virgin until two years ago, at the age of twenty-three. Her first sexual encounter had been with Chad Freeman, a co-ed with her at the University of Nevada, Reno, who'd pursued her for weeks, until she'd finally accepted an invitation to dinner, which led to a series of dates thereafter. When she'd finally agreed to sleep with him, believing she was ready to take that intimate step, the experience had been awkward and one-sided. And their sexual encounters failed to improve for her. Despite wanting more physically, she'd settled for less-than-fulfilling sex.

As their relationship progressed, Chad's attitude toward her changed. He'd grown distrustful, domineering and jealous. Anytime a man looked her way he'd comment that if she didn't dress like a tramp she wouldn't draw so much attention. If she gave any indication that she wanted more sexually, like an orgasm of her own, he'd tell her she was easy.

He'd been a master at mind games, and the possessive relationship had continued until she'd accepted a job as a showgirl at a Reno casino to make some extra money while going to school during the day. Chad's temper had exploded for the first time, and after berating her for flaunting her body in front of other men, he'd demanded she quit her new job.

Done with him controlling her mentally, emotionally and physically, she'd refused his order and broken off their relationship, which only enraged him more. For the next three months he'd stalked her, threatened her and finally attacked her one night after work. Afraid a restraining order wouldn't stop his madness, and having no loved ones to leave behind, she'd packed up her meager belongings and abruptly moved to Oakland to start out fresh, leaving no forwarding address.

Her chest tightened at the awful memories, along with the wave of insecurities that had come in the aftermath of that tumultuous relationship. Diligently pushing those disturbing recollections aside as she'd done hundreds of times before, she focused on her new life in Oakland. She might lead a solitary, monotonous existence, but she was safe here. And that was all that mattered to her. Or so she tried to convince herself during long, lonely nights when she wished she had more to keep her warm than college textbooks and sensual fantasies of a certain blue-eyed, dark-haired Adonis.

But that's all she'd have—private musings and erotic dreams of Noah, because she knew how dangerous it was to let her desires be known, to get involved and allow a man control over her mind and body. Her relationship with Chad had turned into a humiliating experience that had left her second-guessing her longing to be treated like a real woman, to enjoy her body's response to a man's touch.

"Yo, Earth to Natalie," Murphy said, his deep voice penetrating her thoughts. "You've got drinks to deliver and the crowd's getting restless."

Startled that she'd allowed her mind to drift while her order sat waiting, she hustled to load up her tray. "Sorry 'bout that, Murph," she said, slanting him a sheepish look. "Just resting my brain for a few minutes. I had a hellish day at school today."

He smiled, his brown eyes gentle with understanding. "I'm thinking you're spending too much time with your head between those college psycho-babble books and not enough time taking care of yourself."

"I'm fine and it won't happen again," she promised, and headed toward the lounge with her drinks before Murphy could launch into one of his well-meaning lectures about needing more of a life than work and school.

Her classes and studies were her lifeline and what kept her sane and her mind occupied. And she honestly loved her major, which was in social work. Counseling troubled kids was her goal, and she'd even taken on part-time work at a foster-care agency over the past summer months to gain hands-on experience and further her credentials. She'd been where those foster kids were. She knew how it felt being an outsider looking in, and being a number in the system that didn't always work in a child's favor.

She understood what they needed emotionally and wasn't afraid to share her own personal stories to put them at ease.

Minutes later she was lost again in the demands of the patrons. The atmosphere in the bar was casual, and she chatted with the regulars she'd developed a friendly rapport with over the months. It was especially nice that most of the customers that frequented the establishment were blue collar, and a good percentage of them worked in law enforcement, which made for a safe environment in Natalie's way of thinking. Bobby Malone was a detective, and even Noah was a private investigator who worked at his brother's agency, Sommers Investigative Specialists.

She placed a plate of potato skins on a table between a couple on a date and shivered at the thought of Noah uncovering all her secrets. And what about the erotic fantasies she harbored involving him? He'd either be very shocked or very pleased to discover her private thoughts with him in the starring role. Not that he'd ever find out how she truly felt about him.

After nine months of looking over her shoulder, she was just starting to feel safe and secure with her life. The last thing she needed to do was allow sexual urges to lead her astray, despite how much Noah's flirtatious behavior beckoned her to take a chance on him, to be a bit wild, reckless, and adventurous for a change.

It couldn't happen.

She delivered kamikaze shots to a trio of guys in a corner booth, took more orders for drinks and appetizers, refilled bowls of peanuts, cleaned tables and collected generous tips along the way. Once she had the customers in her section of the lounge taken care of for the moment, she headed into the gaming area and stopped at Noah and Bobby's pool table first.

"Hey, boys, I'm getting ready to clock out in about ten minutes." She picked up their empty beer bottles and swiped peanut shells onto her tray. "Can I get either of you a refill before I go?"

Bobby smiled her way and racked up the billiard balls for a new game. "I'll take another Miller."

"You got it." Jotting down his request on her pad of paper, she glanced toward Noah, who was watching her in that wholly masculine way of his that made her pulse race. "How about you?"

He gave his head a quick shake. "No refill for me. I've hit my limit for the night."

Two beers was Noah's max, and she respected that and him for knowing his limit and sticking to it. His older brother, Cole, was the same way, though it had been a while since she'd seen him in Murphy's for an evening out with the guys.

She tipped her head, meeting Noah's striking blue eyes. He was one of the few men who actually looked at her face instead of her chest or body, but she found his stare equally unnerving. And too damn arousing. "Would you like anything else?"

A disarming grin slid into place. "Now, Natalie," he chided in a lazy drawl that did crazy, delightful things to her insides, "you should know better than to ask me a question like that. You know exactly what I'd *like,* but I don't think a date is on the menu.''

She laughed lightly. ''No, it's not.'' The man was an outrageous flirt, and because he'd never made an improper advance toward her, she let herself enjoy his charm while she worked. He made her feel feminine and desired, and while a part of her instinctively curbed those reactions, she couldn't deny that those sensual feelings were still there beneath the surface, struggling to overpower their restraints.

Lord help her if those provocative cravings ever broke free with this man.

Noah chalked his cue stick for the opening break shot, his movements slow, sure, too sexy. ''Then I guess there's nothing else I want tonight.''

Which left every other night ahead wide open, she read in his gaze.

She had to admire his determination. Most men would have given up on her the first time she'd turned down a date. Noah was made of stronger stuff than most.

Noah bent over the pool table to line up his shot and cocked his hip for a better position and leverage. His stance drew her gaze to the muscles along his shoulders and down his back, which flexed with his every movement. The tips of her fingers tingled at the thought of touching all that virile strength, of smoothing her hand down the slope of his spine and testing the heat and texture of his skin.

God, it had been so, so long....

Her throat grew dry and she swallowed hard. A

change in subject was definitely in order. "Where's Cole been lately?" she asked, clearing off a nearby table that had been recently vacated.

A loud, solid *crack* rent the air as the cue ball made contact, sending the rest of the colored balls scattering across the table. Three made it into pockets—two solids and a stripe.

"Solids," Noah called to Bobby, then said to Natalie, "Cole's got something better to do with his evenings than hang out here with us confirmed bachelors."

"Oh, and what's that?" she asked, curious.

He moved around the table, and spying a straight shot into the corner pocket, he lined up his cue. "Spending it with his fiancée, Melodie." He scored another point.

She crumpled up damp cocktail napkins and stuffed them into the empty glasses on her tray. "That's right. Aren't they getting married soon?"

"Next Saturday, actually." He glanced up before making his next shot, his expression heated and hopeful. "Care to accompany me to the wedding?"

There was that temptation again, and she steeled herself against his sensual allure. "Sorry, but I have to work that night."

He hit the cue ball, which barely grazed a solid. He sighed, the sound tinged with the barest hint of defeat. "Can't blame a guy for asking." He moved away from the table to give Bobby his turn, and strolled slowly over to join her where she stood in the corner of the room. "One of these days I might get lucky and you'll say yes."

"Gina would be happy to go with you," she suggested without thinking, and nearly bit off her tongue. While she knew she'd never accept a date with Noah, she hated the idea of him getting close and intimate with anyone else. God, she was pathetic! She had no claim to him, other than her nightly erotic dreams.

He stopped inches away, so close she could feel the warmth of his big body, could smell the scent of his woodsy after-shave. It struck her just how big he was, how tall. How overwhelmingly male in every way. And if he so much as inhaled a deep breath his chest would graze her full breasts and taut nipples.

She held her own breath.

He bent his knees until they were face-to-face, his mouth a kiss away. His dark blue gaze locked with hers, and in a low, rumbling voice he said, "Sweetheart, it's not Gina I'm interested in."

Her legs turned to rubber, and her heart thumped hard and fast, pumping with a need that was almost painful. He hadn't touched her physically, so why did she feel as though he'd caressed her intimately with his hands, from breasts to thighs?

She managed a smile, along with a stubborn tip of her chin. "Then it looks like you'll be attending the affair solo."

He lifted a brow at the subtle challenge in her tone, but before he could say anything more, or seduce her completely senseless with his eyes and voice, she slipped past him. Shaken, she made her way back to the bar, asked Gina to deliver Bobby's bottle of beer, and received the okay from Murphy to leave for the evening.

She headed to the storeroom to get her jacket and purse, grateful that her shift was over. And so very disappointed that she couldn't bring herself to say *yes* to Noah.

"BETTER LUCK NEXT TIME, buddy," Bobby said, and slapped Noah's back in a show of sympathetic male camaraderie.

"I wouldn't count on it." Noah pulled his gaze from where Natalie had disappeared down a short hallway to the storeroom, certain his luck wasn't going to improve anytime soon where she was concerned. "Melodie put a curse on me, and I'm beginning to think she's a true witch." His tone was wry, but the words his soon-to-be sister-in-law had spoken to him months ago haunted him now.

Bobby chuckled and continued their game of pool, sinking a striped ball into the side pocket. "Why do you say that?"

Thrusting his fingers through his thick hair, Noah alternated his gaze from his friend to the back hall, waiting for Natalie to reappear. "One day a while back when Melodie was trying to get my brother's attention, she took her frustration out on me. Not only did she call me a rake, but she also said she hoped I'd find a woman I absolutely had to have, and that woman makes *me* work for *her* affection." *Some*

woman who'll reform you and your playboy ways,
she'd added.

His stomach knotted at the recollection. At the time
he'd been amused with Melodie's comment and had
responded with a teasing ''It's a novel thought, isn't
it?'' But now that he was in that exact situation, trying
to get the attention of a woman who aroused and intrigued him beyond his normal span of interest, his
predicament wasn't so funny.

Natalie had gotten under his skin and kept him
coming back to Murphy's on a regular basis. For
months now he'd flirted with her, trying to coax her
into a date, but she always turned down his invita-
tions, despite the subtle longing he'd seen shimmering
in her eyes. Initially, he'd been baffled because no
woman had ever resisted his advances for so long,
and admittedly his male ego had taken a direct hit.
Then she became a challenge to him, and now an
obsession.

One he couldn't seem to shake.

And at the moment, his randy body was making
that fixation known. Just standing near enough to
touch and kiss her had made his blood run hot and
his groin tighten in awareness. It had taken every
ounce of willpower not to taste her parted lips, and
judging by the desire he'd seen flash across her features, he knew she hadn't been immune to their close
proximity, either.

Undoubtedly, he was highly attracted to her, but it
was more than just her incredible body and their sizzling chemistry that drew him. While she was out-

wardly intelligent, gorgeous and sweet, there was more to her than met his trained eye, a vulnerability he'd glimpsed a time or two. She was very private, very reserved. And there were emotional barriers she erected that gave him the impression she was hiding something deeper than feigned disinterest.

"My game."

Noah turned around and frowned at Bobby, who was grinning triumphantly. "Huh?"

"The game's over. I won." His friend leaned a hip against the pool table and shook his head. "Man, you really do have it bad for her if you can't concentrate on a game of pool."

It would be ridiculous to deny the obvious, so Noah didn't even try.

Bobby jutted his chin toward the front of the establishment. "She's on her way out, Romeo. Here's your chance to impress her with your chivalrous charm and open the door for her—which in turn might open the door for you, if you know what I mean."

Noah certainly did. "Thank you, Dr. Ruth," he joked, and made his way to the front of the bar, beating Natalie to the entrance by three paces. He opened the door for her, and she glanced up at him in startled surprise.

She adjusted the strap of her purse on her shoulder and smoothed her hand along the jacket draped over her arm. "Are you leaving, too?"

"Sure am." He waved his hand for her to precede him, then followed, falling into step beside her on the sidewalk, welcoming the cool evening breeze on his too-warm skin. "Actually, leaving the same time as you is a shameless ploy to walk you to your car."

Abruptly, she stopped, a frown marring her brow, though there was no denying the awareness in the depths of her eyes. "I can make it to my vehicle on my own just fine. I don't need an escort, Noah."

"I didn't say you did," he replied gently, trying to put her at ease and lighten the moment between them. "This is solely for *my* pleasure."

Her tense shoulders loosened up, and the corner of her mouth twitched with a hint of a smile. Still, she hesitated, seemingly divided between letting him accompany her or telling him to get lost.

Not wanting to lose the ground he'd just gained, he opted for a bit of humor. "You know, if it makes you feel any better, I don't bite."

She visibly shivered and slipped into her lightweight jacket. "Oh, yeah? How can I be so certain of that?"

She was eyeing him in a way that was more playful than suspicious, and he took his cue from her. "Because if I did bite, I would have taken a nibble or two out of you by now." Without thinking of the consequences, he reached out and lifted her shoulder-length blond hair from under the collar of her jacket.

Her breath caught as his fingers delved through the warm, silky mass at the nape of her neck and his thumbs grazed the soft skin beneath her jaw. Time seemed suspended as their gazes met, hers reflecting a flare of heat that burned through his veins. People walked past them, but he was oblivious to anything but her.

It was the first time he'd touched her in any way, and the connection was inherently intimate and wholly sensual. Her lips were parted, and he ached to pull her into his arms, lower his mouth to hers and claim the kiss he'd forfeited earlier in the bar.

As if sensing his intent, she stepped back, and he automatically dropped his hands away and cleared his throat. Before she could flat-out turn him down again, he lightly grasped her elbow and ushered her toward the parking lot, which was located across the street from Murphy's. "Come on, I'm walking you to your car, and I'm not taking no for an answer so don't waste your breath arguing."

She relaxed and smiled, and they walked by the other storefronts along the street to the intersection.

"You know, we could consider this nice, casual stroll to your car a first date," he suggested, only half joking. He'd take a date with her any way he could get one.

She thrust her hands deep into her jacket pockets and slanted him a sly look. "Ah, so you *do* have an ulterior motive other than seeing me safely to my car."

"A very harmless motive, I swear." He held up his hands and attempted to look innocent. "We could head over to Starbucks and get a coffee and just talk about the weather if you'd like."

An incredulous burst of laughter escaped her. "The weather? Are you serious?"

He shrugged and winked at her. "I wouldn't want our first date to be *too* personal."

She chewed on her full bottom lip, looking torn, then said, "Noah, I can't."

The light at the intersection was red, and Noah pushed the button to give them the right of way, unwilling to give up on her so easily this time. "Not even one coffee? I promise no hand-holding or kissing."

That made her smile again, but her next words shot down his hopes. "I'm sorry, but I've got a big test on Monday I need to study for."

"We could have a study date," he suggested. "There are a few things I'm really good at teaching."

"I'm not going to touch that one," she murmured huskily. Hearing someone approach from behind, she glanced over her shoulder briefly, then back at Noah. "You don't give up, do you?"

Something in her expression had changed in those few seconds, and there was now a troubled glint in her eyes that snagged his attention, but he didn't understand its source. Wanting to soothe her sudden anxiety, he picked up her hand and drew a lazy pattern on her palm with his index finger. "I'd give up if you told me to get lost and meant it."

She stared at him, then shook her head, sending her soft blond waves brushing across her shoulders. "You're way too—"

"Irresistible?" He graced her with one of his enticing grins that never failed to score him extra points with the opposite sex.

The light changed to green, the cars on the street stopped, and they stepped off the curb to cross, severing the contact of their joined hands. "I was thinking more along the lines of *persistent.*"

He laughed. "Hey, I do have a *few* faults."

She seemed distracted enough not to hear or appreciate his attempt at humor. The footsteps behind them sounded closer, and this time when she looked behind them, Noah saw her stiffen, then she hastened her steps.

He lengthened his stride to keep up. She'd piqued not only his concern but his P.I. instincts, and he glanced back, too, and saw a man about ten yards away, wearing a sweatshirt, jeans and a baseball cap. The lighting in the area was adequate, but the bill of the cap cast a shadow over half his face. The hairs on the back of Noah's neck prickled with awareness, and every investigative intuition he possessed came to full alert.

By the time they reached the other side of the street, she was nearly jogging, trying to escape a danger he didn't understand. His only thought was to grab her to keep her close and make sure she felt safe with him. Whatever had set her off, there was no way he'd let anything or anyone harm her.

Latching onto her upper arm, he forced her to stop. The street lamp overhead illuminated the sheer panic etched on her face, and he felt her tremble in fear. His gut tightened in unease. "Natalie, what's wrong?"

Her gaze shifted over his shoulder to whoever was

approaching them, and her complexion paled. "Oh, God, *No!*" she said on a helpless moan and tried to tug her arm free from his grasp so she could bolt.

He refused to release her, knowing in her near-hysterical state she wasn't thinking straight and could hurt herself. He wanted to shake her out of her stupor but didn't want to scare her even more. He decided on verbal force. "Dammit, Natalie, talk to me!" he growled in a low tone.

"It's *him,*" she said on a soft, keening cry, her eyes wide and filled with alarm.

She wasn't making any coherent sense, nor was she giving him any information he could act upon. "It's *who?*"

She shook her head frantically, and gripping his shirt in her hands, she pulled him into a small alcove built into the back doorway of a shop.

Stunned and confused by her abrupt action, he braced his hands on the door behind her to catch himself before his body slammed into hers. "What the hell's going on?" He turned his head to get a better look at the person who'd sent her into such a tailspin, but she wrapped her arms around his neck and fisted her fingers tight in his hair, which kept him in place.

Her eyes pleaded with him to help her, to do as she requested. *"Just kiss me,"* she demanded in a hoarse voice.

Before he could say another word, she crushed her soft lips to his.

2

FOR AS MANY TIMES AS NOAH had fantasized about this moment with Natalie, he'd never once imagined he'd be kissing her during a crisis. Neither had he expected her to be the aggressor. No, he'd always envisioned their first kiss as a slow, sensual, erotic exploration. Him coaxing her passion to the surface at a leisurely pace, and her gradually surrendering.

This reckless embrace went beyond a sweet, lingering kiss and went straight for fast, deep and blistering hot, as well as wild and consuming. She clung to him as if she wanted to crawl into his skin and be a part of him, plastering her soft, lush curves along the length of his body in a way his long-denied libido couldn't ignore. The fingers she'd thrust through his hair flexed for a better hold and she angled his mouth for greater pressure, sealing their lips so tightly he was certain he'd bruise her.

She didn't seem to care. Desperation poured off her in waves as their tongues mated in a wild, illicit dance of seduction, despite the danger he sensed around them. He tasted her panic, felt her fear, even as she kissed him with an erotic intensity that left him reeling. And every time he tried to pull away she grew more frantic, which in turn increased the depth and heat and friction of their mouths and bodies.

He didn't like having his back exposed to whatever element had frightened her, but he'd never in his life been held with such force and need by a woman—a woman intent on either using him as diversionary tactic, or a shield to protect her from harm. He swore he'd keep her safe even as he fought the drugging pleasure of having her so willing and eager in his arms.

Christ. Her feverish kiss and their intimate embrace sent conflicting signals through his brain and body. His muscles were tensed and braced for action, yet he was hard and aching where his erection pressed against her belly. He groaned low in his throat as desire mingled with arousal, and he struggled with wanting this, wanting *her,* but knowing the circumstances were all wrong.

It seemed an eternity had passed, though in reality only a few seconds had ticked by, when Noah finally gained the upper hand and pried her lips from his, then pulled her arms from his neck. She whimpered at the loss of contact, her entire body shaking uncontrollably. She was breathing hard, and tears of despair shone in her bright, wide eyes as she looked up at him.

He pressed two fingers to her still-damp lips to keep her quiet until he got a better feel for their predicament. "I won't let anything hurt you," he promised in a low, gravelly voice.

Keeping her covered with his body, he leaned back

and peered around the alcove to see if there was anyone waiting for them. He saw a few pedestrians stroll-
ing along the sidewalk, but not the guy in the baseball
cap who had seemingly set her off.

He returned his attention to Natalie, needing to
know what she'd seen and what had threatened her
so badly. But first he had to calm her, and he tried to
do so by rubbing his hands along her arms. "Nobody's there, Natalie. You're safe with me."

"I'll never be safe." Her voice caught on a hysterical sob as she shook her head wildly. "He won't
go away!"

She pushed at his chest, shoving him away, and the
unexpected assault took him off guard and he stumbled back a step. This time she alluded his grasp, and
before he could intercept her she was dashing back
across the street toward Murphy's. The signal at the
corner was red, and he yelled at her to stop. She didn't
listen, just kept running to escape.

From what, he still didn't know.

He started after her, cursing at his inability to control the bizarre situation and her rash actions. Before
he could reach the street, an oncoming car slammed
on its brakes to avoid hitting her. But the driver was
going too fast, and Natalie wasn't paying attention.

He watched in horror, shouting a hoarse warning
as the vehicle skidded long and hard, striking Natalie
just before the car came to a jarring stop. The impact
sent her flying, and she landed on her side a few feet
away, her golden blond hair tousled around her head,

her arms at an awkward angle, and her body completely lifeless.

Stunned, Noah raced furiously toward her, yelling at the people pouring out of nearby shops and eateries to dial 911 and get an ambulance there immediately. He dropped to the ground beside her, mindless of the sharp pain that shot through his knees. Mindless of anything except the churning in his gut and the metallic taste of fear in his mouth. He pressed two fingers to the pulse point at her neck, and exhaled a sigh of relief when he felt a thready but noticeable beat. She was alive, and that's all he cared about.

A crowd gathered around him, and the driver made his way to Noah's side, babbling about not seeing her in the street until it was too late. Ignoring him, he gently eased Natalie to her back and began a check for injuries, running his hands from her shoulders, down her arms, and along her thighs and legs. Opening her jacket, he skimmed his fingers over her collarbone, ribs and hips, and found nothing broken.

Her jacket had protected her from getting any scrapes along her arms, but she had a nasty cut on her cheek oozing blood that hopefully wouldn't leave a scar. Her face was drained of color, her lips were white and cool to the touch, and she looked so damn vulnerable.

''The paramedics are on their way,'' someone called from behind him.

Grateful for that bit of news, he held Natalie's slender, cold hand in his bigger, warmer one and silently urged the ambulance to hurry.

"Police coming through," a deep, distinct voice ordered. "Please step back from the injured party."

Bobby's authoritative tone reached Noah, and he glanced up to see his friend flashing his badge and doing his best to make the throng of curious onlookers back away to give them breathing room. When Bobby saw that it was him, he immediately hunkered down beside Noah.

"Oh, shit, it's Natalie," he said, sounding as shocked as Noah felt. "I had no idea. We heard the accident from inside Murphy's and I came out to see what happened. Is she okay?"

"I'm not sure," Noah said, hating that he didn't know more. "She's out cold and hasn't regained consciousness yet."

Automatically, Bobby tested the arteries in her wrist. "Her pulse is steady, so that's a good sign."

Noah nodded in agreement but knew there could be more damage that they couldn't see. "Do me a favor? Take care of the driver for me. He's really shaken up. It wasn't his fault. She ran out in front of his car when he had the right of way."

Bobby's dark brows lifted in surprise at that bit of news. "She was with you, wasn't she?" he asked, confused. "How did this happen, anyway?"

A weary sigh escaped Noah. "Long story, and I'll fill you in on the details as soon as Natalie is taken care of."

"Fair enough," his friend said, respecting Noah's wishes and knowing he'd get the full blow-by-blow later.

Bobby went to do his bidding, and Noah remained beside Natalie, refusing to leave her for any reason. He smoothed her hair away from her face and whispered encouraging words to her, along with the plea for her to open her eyes, all to no avail.

He pressed his lips to the tips of her fingers, wishing he could breath life and energy back into her body. He couldn't remember a time when he'd ever felt so helpless, so filled with dread, not even when his parents divorced or when his father was killed in the line of duty. The latter had been a tragic experience for him and his brother and sister, but he'd managed to compartmentalize his pain with a carefree, easygoing façade. It was a strategy that had served him well in life up until this moment.

It hit him hard that this woman had the ability to cripple him emotionally. Over the course of the months he'd been pursuing her, she'd somehow worked her way into his heart, in a way he'd never, ever anticipated. The thought of losing her tore at his insides and made him physically ill.

Finally, he heard the sound of sirens, and within a minute the ambulance was parked and the paramedics were ushering him away from Natalie and taking over. One of the EMTs asked him what had happen, and Noah told them what they needed to know so they'd have better insight to possible injuries.

Still unconscious, Natalie was transferred to a cot, covered with blankets and wheeled to the ambulance for transport to the nearest hospital. Noah followed, refusing to let her out of his sight. They hefted her into the back of the unit, and Noah flashed his P.I. badge to avoid any flack and said, "I'm going with her."

Nobody argued as he climbed inside and settled on the bench seat opposite Natalie's cot. One EMT went to work hooking her up to an IV, then taking her blood pressure, while another man checked to see if her pupils dilated when he flashed a spot of light in her eyes.

Bobby came up to the back of the ambulance, his gaze showing compassion and concern. "I'm going to take some eyewitness reports, then I'll met you at the hospital."

"Thanks," Noah said with a nod. "I'll call Cole on the way and let him know what happened."

The dual doors closed, and the ambulance took off, lights flashing and sirens wailing as they sped through the city to the hospital.

It was the longest ride of Noah's life.

NOAH PACED RESTLESSLY in the hospital waiting room, surrounded by Cole, Melodie and Bobby. It had been three hours since Natalie had been admitted, and other than a few vague updates that didn't satisfy Noah, they still didn't know her final prognosis. The wait was excruciating, and he was eternally grateful that he had the support of his friend and family to keep him company.

Scrubbing a hand along his tense jaw, he exhaled in frustration. The last time he, Cole and Melodie had been in a hospital had been five months ago when their sister, Joelle, had gone into labor. Back then their presence in a medical facility had been a happy, joyful event as they'd welcomed an eight-pound, three-ounce baby girl Jo and Dean had named Jennifer. But today, the mood was somber and grim as the four of them waited for the doctor to give them an update on Natalie's condition.

He took a drink of the dark coffee Melodie had purchased down at the cafeteria for them, the bitter taste adding to the regrets and guilt swirling within him. "If only I'd tried harder to stop her," he muttered, speaking his thoughts out loud.

"Quit blaming yourself for something that was out of your control, Noah," Cole said, his tone understanding. He was the same old voice of reason he'd been since their father died. "It won't change what happened."

Regardless, he felt partially responsible for the accident. Hadn't he told Natalie that she was safe with him? He'd done a crummy job of protecting her.

He transferred his gaze to Bobby, who sat on a tweed chair, his dark hair as mussed as Noah's. "Are you sure nobody at the scene saw anything out of the ordinary?"

"I'm positive." Bobby took a swallow from his own cup of coffee, wincing at the strong taste that even a dose of sugar hadn't been able to tone down. "Everyone I spoke with either witnessed her running without paying attention to the light signal, or they didn't catch the accident until after it happened."

Noah pitched his empty foam cup into a nearby

wastebasket. "I was hoping that someone at least saw that guy in the sweatshirt and baseball cap I told you about."

"Nope," Bobby said, dashing his hopes.

"Did he do something to attract attention or threaten her?" Melodie asked, joining in on the conversation. Having worked with Cole on a few cases, she was perceptive when it came to picking up on details.

"No. He was just walking behind us. He didn't say anything or make any hostile moves toward us." They'd been over the scene a dozen times but hadn't come up with clues that explained Natalie's strange behavior. She was the only one who could give them those missing pieces to the puzzle. "But whoever he is, without a doubt he's what set Natalie off."

"Then we'll just have to wait until we can talk to Natalie and find out who the guy is," Bobby replied pragmatically. "The way things look right now, the department can't even start an investigation on the guy, not unless Natalie gives us more information to go on."

Noah shoved both hands, palms out, into the back pockets of his jeans. "I'm sure she'll cooperate once she's feeling better." At least he was hopeful she'd share more information than she had earlier.

Forty minutes later, a doctor in green scrubs came out of the double doors separating the waiting room from the staff.

"Who here is a relative of Ms. Hastings?" he asked, adjusting his wire-rimmed glasses on the bridge of his nose as he glanced around at the people in the area.

Noah automatically stepped forward. "I am."

The lie slipped out with ease. He didn't know if she had any family in the area, and hadn't found anything in her purse to indicate so. He needed to know her status, wanted to make sure whatever threat she'd seen didn't make its way any closer to her. And the only way he could assure her safety was to appoint himself as her full-time bodyguard until this mess was straightened out. Which meant lying when necessary.

He shook the other man's hand. "I'm her fiancé," he added, just for an extended measure of believability. He caught Melodie's big, rounded eyes and Cole's raised brow from behind the doctor, and ignored them both. "How is Natalie?"

"She's in stable condition right now," the other man said, clasping his hands in front of him. "She has no life-threatening injuries but did suffer a concussion when her head hit the ground. She's regained consciousness a few times, so that's a good sign."

A huge blanket of worry lifted from Noah's shoulders. "So she's going to be okay?"

"Physically, she'll be sore and bruised for a few days, but she'll recover just fine," the doctor reassured him. "Emotionally and mentally, though, we're a bit concerned. We ran tests and X rays and did an MRI just to be sure we ruled out anything serious, but it does appear that she's suffering some memory loss. She only remembers bits and pieces leading up to the accident, and it's apparent that part of her memory is blocked.''

"Are you saying she has amnesia?" he asked incredulously.

"The technical term is 'retrograde amnesia,'" the doctor clarified. "It's quite common with people who have sustained head injuries, or have suffered from something traumatic leading up to an accident."

That certainly qualified in Natalie's case. Noah glanced in disbelief at the trio listening in on the conversation, then back to the calm, patient doctor standing in front of him. "So, how long does this amnesia last?"

"It can last anywhere from hours, to days, to weeks. The amnesia in this case is very selective, and there is usually a full recovery in time. We'll be keeping her overnight for further observation, but I do suggest that once she's discharged from the hospital she isn't left alone until she's feeling confident about her surroundings and the people in her life."

"That's not a problem," Noah said abruptly, and wove another lie to keep her safe from potential harm. "We live together."

"Very good, then." The doctor smiled pleasantly. "When you see her, don't pressure her to remember things, because that can cause her more stress and can possibly suppress her memories deeper. Just let her remember things as they come to her, and in her own time."

"Can I see her?" he asked hopefully.

"She's resting right now—"

"I swear I won't bother her," he interrupted quickly, desperately. "I just need to see for myself that she's okay."

The older man glanced around the waiting room, his gaze briefly settling on Bobby, Cole and Melodie. "Are there any other family members here?"

"No, her family doesn't live in the area." The fibs kept getting easier and easier to fabricate, and he was grateful that nobody interfered.

The doctor hesitated a moment, then gave a succinct nod of his head. "That's fine. In fact, I can have one of the nurses bring in a cot to her room for you if you'd like to stay the night. That way, she can wake up to a familiar face."

"That would be great." He shook the other man's hand again, appreciating the opportunity to be close to her. "Thank you."

After issuing goodbyes to his brother, Melodie and Bobby, and promising to let them all know what he found out when he was able to question Natalie, he followed a nurse to Natalie's private room.

"I'll be back with a cot and extra blankets for you," the nurse said, then left him alone with Natalie.

He stepped inside the small hospital room, his eyes instantly drawn to the sleeping form on the bed. A lightweight blanket covered her up to her chest, and she was still hooked to an IV. The soft blip of a unit monitoring her heart and breathing told him that she was, indeed, stabilized. The color was back in her face, and a butterfly bandage covered the cut on her cheek, which hadn't required stitches, thank goodness.

The awful tightness he'd been experiencing in his chest since the accident finally eased. Pulling a chair close to her bedside, he sat down, leaned forward and placed his hand over Natalie's, just to have some kind of connection to her.

His fingers felt the pulse in her wrist, and he watched the steady rise and fall of her chest and the fluttering of her eyelids as she dreamed. Her lips were parted slightly, and remembering their kiss, he was determined that their next one would be much softer, much sweeter, with nothing but desire and mutual hunger between them.

His cot was delivered, along with some water for him to drink. Nurses periodically came into the room to check on her, and he made it clear that he wasn't going to leave Natalie's side until she awakened.

And as the minutes ticked by, one concern preyed heavily on his mind. Would she even remember him when she woke up?

HER THROAT FELT PARCHED and she was so thirsty.

Natalie pulled herself from her deep, dreamless sleep and pried her eyes open. She blinked, focusing on her surroundings, recalling with a startling jolt that she'd been in an accident and was in the hospital. She shivered as she caught sight of the equipment and wires hooked up to her sore, aching body, and inhaled an antiseptic scent that tickled her nose. The back of her skull hurt, too, and she had a headache to match.

She glanced at the clock on the wall in front of her and saw it was six-thirty—in the morning, she assumed.

She closed her eyes again, this time trying to recall any small detail of being hit by a car, but all she remembered was gaining consciousness in the hospital after the fact and wondering what the heck was going on. Last night she'd felt so bewildered and confused, and her head had felt as though something had stampeded through her brain. Exhaustion had finally claimed her, which had been a blessed relief since she hadn't been able to make sense of anything.

It seemed a good night's rest hadn't made any difference, and she couldn't stop the niggling sense of unease that trickled through her. Before her anxiety could spring into full-blown panic, she calmed herself with the knowledge that she'd been through a traumatic accident and the certainty that things would become clearer as the day progressed.

A soft, snoring sound pulled her from her disturbing thoughts. With a frown, she turned her head, glanced down and found a man slumped forward in a chair at the side of her bed, his dark head and brawny arms resting on the mattress near her hip.

Another snuffling sound escaped him, and she smiled, recognizing that tousled sable hair and the strong, gorgeous profile as Noah's. It appeared he'd fallen asleep while watching over her, and the caring gesture warmed her deep inside.

A brief recollection flashed inside her head, of Noah's lips on hers and a wild, deep kiss unlike anything she'd ever indulged in. She *knew* Noah, and along with that certainty came the knowledge that he made her feel safe, secure and desired. But she had no idea where he fit into her life. Was he her boyfriend? Lover? Friend? Judging by the awareness and intimate longing swirling within her, she was guessing that he was much more than a casual acquaintance.

Stretching her arm out, she gently threaded her fingers through his hair, the thick strands cool and silky to the touch. She caressed her hand along the dark, bristly whiskers on his cheek and jaw, trying to recall if she'd ever been abraded by that sexy morning stubble. His lips were parted and looked so warm and soft. So inviting. She couldn't resist testing the feel of them for herself, and she wasn't disappointed in the silky, seductive texture her fingertips encountered.

His lashes drifted open as he gradually awakened, his dark blue eyes at first unfocused. God, he was so sinfully sensual, so deliciously good-looking, he literally took her breath away.

The charming grin she expected to see never appeared. Instead, he slowly lifted his head and stared at her cautiously, warily searching her gaze as if he wasn't sure what to expect from *her*. Odd, she thought.

Regardless, his presence soothed her, grounded her, and she was grateful that she hadn't woken up alone. "Hi, there," she said, her voice husky from slumber and thirst.

He swallowed hard, then finally graced her with

that sexy smile that never failed to jump-start her pulse. That exciting tingling through her veins was an incredibly nice way to greet the morning, though she couldn't ever recall waking up with this man next to her.

Not that it had or hadn't happened. She just couldn't...*remember*. Her mind felt muddled, foggy and disoriented, and the inability to grasp any kind of clear recollection of *them* frustrated her.

"Hi, yourself, sweetheart," he murmured, his tone low and rough.

Sweetheart. Yeah, she definitely liked the sound of that. And she knew that he'd used that sentiment with her before.

He straightened in his seat, then stretched his arms over his head to loosen the kinks that had no doubt cramped parts of his body due to his awkward sleeping position. Muscles flexed beneath his T-shirt and along his arms as he arched his back and reached high. He groaned in relief, and she enjoyed every bit of the male display.

"You snore," she said in amusement.

"I'm sorry." He cringed at that bit of information, instantly contrite. "Did I wake you?"

"No, actually it was a cute snore and not at all obnoxious."

He laughed, the rumbling sound sending a pleasant vibration along her nerve endings. "Well, it's certainly good to know that *you* think my snores are cute, but don't tell anyone else because, for one thing, I'll never hear the end of it and, for another, it'll be a huge blow to my masculinity.''

''Don't worry, your secret's safe with me.'' She smiled, curious to know if they shared any other private intimacies. ''I need something to drink. Is there any water?''

''Sure is.'' He raised the top of her mattress so she was sitting up, then filled a plastic glass on the tray next to her bed. Bringing the straw to her lips, he watched her take a drink, his concerned gaze roaming over her face. ''You sound better than I'd expected this morning, but how are you *really* feeling?''

She swallowed one last gulp of cool water, relieving her dry, scratchy throat. ''My head is throbbing and I feel bruised, battered and achy. Like I got hit by a car.''

He chuckled lightly at her wry tone and tipped his head. ''You remember?''

''Not much, if anything at all.'' She sighed and settled back against her pillows. ''Actually, one of the nurses told me what happened when I asked last night. That's how I know. I'm still kind of sketchy on the details, though.''

He took a long drink of water from her glass and set it aside. ''That's okay. It'll eventually come to you. I'm just glad to see your beautiful eyes are wide open and clear. You gave us all quite a scare.''

''Us all?''

Nodding, he perched his hip on the mattress next to her waist and placed her hand between his. His thumb drew lazy patterns over her knuckles. ''Me, my brother, Melodie, Bobby, and everyone at Murphy's.''

She thought hard to place who those people were. Struck with a sudden dull ache at her temple, she pressed her fingers against the sore spot. ''The names are familiar, but why can't I place their faces?'' she asked, annoyed with her inability to do so.

He hesitated, his gentle caresses stopping. Then he asked very carefully, ''Didn't the doctor tell you?''

By the tone of his voice and the troubled look marring his brows, she was certain she wasn't going to enjoy what he had to say. ''Tell me what?''

He released a deep breath. Now that the issue had been brought up, it was obvious that he felt obligated to carry it through. ''About your amnesia.''

''Amnesia?'' Her voice rose to an incredulous pitch, and she experienced an adrenaline rush of distress. ''But I remember *you*.'' Which was why she hadn't been overly alarmed at the other little things she couldn't recollect. But now that he'd used the word *amnesia,* her lack of recall made more sense, not that she liked it one bit.

''And thank God for that.'' He tenderly brushed her hair away from her cheek, his fingers lingering on her skin. ''But there are other things you might *not* remember.''

Well, she certainly couldn't argue with his statement. Stunned, she could only shake her head in wonder and fear. How strange it was not to recall certain parts of your life, yet know other things so instinctively. Like her inexplicable emotional and physical connection to Noah.

"Tell me what the doctor told you," she asked, and listened to him explain her level of amnesia, and that while she might be able to remember certain aspects of her past and current life, other things might not be clear at all.

She shook her head in shock. "Is this retrograde amnesia permanent?"

"Not according to the doctor," he reassured her. "You suffered a huge trauma when you hit your head, and he said that you'll start remembering things in bits and pieces over the course of the next few weeks or months. He's confident that you'll have a full recovery in time."

She shivered as a chill rippled through her. "But in the meantime, I've only got half a memory? How frightening is that?"

He gave her hand a tender squeeze. "I know it has to be scary, but I promise I'll be here for you."

Knowing she could count on Noah brought her immense comfort, because at the moment she was feeling incredibly alone and vulnerable. "Thank you."

"I wouldn't have it any other way." He bent close and brushed a kiss on her cheek.

His lips were warm and sensual, the scent of him musky and all male. His morning stubble lightly chafed her skin, eliciting a stirring of desire in her blood. Her heart beat hard and fast in her chest, and she was surprised that the monitor she was hooked up to didn't go haywire. When he lifted his head again and met her gaze, his eyes were dark and intense.

She exhaled a slow breath as they stared at each other. She craved and wanted this man in inexplicable ways that defied her current state of mind, and all she knew for certain was that the feeling was honest and true. She trusted her instincts where Noah was concerned, because, for now, her gut intuition was all she had to depend on.

A nurse walked into the room, shattering the intimate moment between them. Noah sat back in his chair as the woman came up to the side of her bed and started adjusting the IV drip. She wore a pastel smock, and the badge hanging around her neck identified her as Shirley Richards, RN.

"You're awake," she said pleasantly, and smiled at Natalie. "How are you feeling this morning?"

"As good as can be expected."

The nurse nodded in understanding. "I'll give you another dose of medication to help with the aches and pains. You'll be sore for a few days, but you're darn lucky that you didn't sustain any internal injuries." She wrapped a blood pressure cuff around her upper arm and pumped it full of air.

As Shirley took her vitals, she glanced across the bed to Noah, then back at Natalie. "You've got yourself quite a fiancé there," she said genuinely. "He was determined to stay with you and has been by your side all night long waiting for you to wake up."

Her eyes widened as she was dealt another dose of shock to deal with. Her *fiancé?* She and Noah were *engaged?* She snuck a peek at her left hand and saw no evidence of an engagement ring but knew that didn't mean anything at all. Undoubtedly, this man was part of her life in some capacity, and when Noah didn't deny or correct the woman's comment, she had no choice but to believe it was true.

And belonging to Noah wasn't an unpleasant thought at all.

"I'm thinking you might need to use the rest room, yes?" Shirley asked once she'd written her numbers down on the chart in front of her bed.

Natalie smiled sheepishly. "That would be nice."

"You should be okay to get up on your own, but I'll be here to help you the first time, just to make sure your legs are steady and you don't get light-headed. And then there's all the IV stuff that can get in your way." The nurse transferred her professional gaze to Noah. "Can you give us about fifteen minutes to do the girl stuff?"

"Sure." A wry grin canted the corner of his mouth and he stood. "I need to use the men's room myself."

He winked at Natalie and turned for the door. She watched him walk out, eyes drawn to his wide shoulders, his strong, lean body and his confident swagger. No matter how she racked her brain trying to recall something as important as an engagement, her mind remained frustratingly blank.

Regardless of her unreliable memory, one thrilling, exciting thought took precedence: this gorgeous, breathtakingly sexy man was all hers.

3

AFTER TAKING CARE OF personal business, Noah washed his hands, then splashed cool water on his face, trying like hell to push away the guilt eating at his conscience. He dried the dampness from his skin with a paper towel and shoved his fingers through his hair in a paltry attempt to tame his unruly morning hair.

Natalie believed he was her fiancé. When the nurse had made that announcement, he'd witnessed Natalie's surprised expression and had held his breath, waiting for her to ask him if it was true. Much to his relief she didn't question the woman's casually tossed words, which saved him from outright lying to Natalie's face. For now.

Bracing his hands on the edge of the porcelain sink, he stared at his reflection in the rest room mirror, noting the lines of exhaustion at the corners of his eyes. Undoubtedly, he was lying by omission, because he planned to use the fiancé pretense to his advantage, to remain as close to her as possible so he could protect her until he nailed the source of her fears the night before. And he knew there would be more fabrications as they became necessary and until she fully regained her memory—all for her own good. For him, it was one hundred percent a safety issue.

He suspected she didn't remember the threat that had scared her, and that made her even more defenseless and too damned vulnerable to the guy she'd run away from. He was beginning to think she was the target of a stalker. What else could explain the hysterical words Natalie had spoken last night before getting hit by the car? *I'll never be safe. He won't go away.*

Right now, with her amnesia, she didn't have the advantage of *knowing* something was wrong, and her instincts might be skewed by memory loss. Her vulnerability put her too much at risk for another encounter that might turn hostile.

And there was no way he'd allow anything else to harm her, not if he could help it.

He left the rest room and stopped at the vending machine in the waiting area. Buying a roll of the strongest mints available, he promptly tossed three of the peppermint Life Savers into his mouth and chewed. While he waited a few more minutes before returning to Natalie's room, he came up with a game plan. He'd ask her casual, no-pressure kinds of questions and see what she did and didn't recollect. He refused to feed her any information or outright tell her the truth about what had led up to the accident, because if she didn't remember, he knew it would only cause her panic and paranoia.

He popped three more mints for good measure, and when he arrived back in her room, she was settled back in bed with a breakfast tray on the small table in front of her. She was still wearing her hospital gown, but her hair had been combed and was smoothed back behind her ears.

She glanced from her meal to him and wrinkled her nose in distaste. "Blech."

He chuckled as he came up beside her. "That bad, huh?"

"While I can't recall what my favorite breakfast food is, I'm sure this isn't it. Watery scrambled eggs, oatmeal that looks like paste, and dry, cold toast." She indicated each item on her tray with a point of her finger. "The only thing that looks worth eating is the fresh fruit."

He had to agree that her breakfast didn't look at all appetizing. "Then eat the fruit and drink your apple juice, and I'll try to sneak in something good later."

She grinned. "How about a pepperoni pizza?"

He chuckled at her enthusiasm, glad to see she was quickly gaining back her energy. "A big ol' pizza box is a bit obvious, don't you think? That'll have to wait until you're home."

"Home?"

The frown creasing her brows told him that she was having a hard time placing where she lived. Which was perfect for him. "My place. We just moved in together."

"Oh." The one word escaped on a breathy note of sound.

He played his cards very cautiously, not wanting

to upset her in any way. "Do you have a problem with that?"

"Well, no, not really." She shrugged. "I mean, if we're engaged, that would make sense."

She was so trusting that he had to push aside another wave of guilt that assaulted him—and remind himself that it was the only way he could keep her safe.

She sighed softly. "I just feel like I'm learning who I am all over again. Or at least parts of who I am."

"That's how it'll be with certain aspects of your memory, according to the doctor." Since she wasn't digging into her breakfast, he filched a grape from the compote and lifted it to her mouth. When her lips automatically parted, he slipped the piece of fruit inside. "We'll do lots of talking and that might spark those repressed parts of your memory."

While her mouth was currently occupied, he casually brought up another subject, wanting to know what she might recall about her past. "Do you want me to contact someone in your family to let them know about your accident?"

"I don't have any family," she said automatically.

Surprised, he asked, "You remember *that?*"

"Yeah, I do," she said, equally stunned by the knowledge. "You were testing me, weren't you?"

As her fiancé, he should have known about her family, and was grateful that she saw his question as a way of testing her mind and memory. That would definitely work in his favor to get information from her. "Yeah, I was. What else do you remember?"

She plucked up a wedge of cantaloupe, slipped it into her mouth and thought for a moment while she chewed. "I remember that my parents died when I was about five in a house fire and I grew up in foster homes."

Oh, wow, he thought, blown away by her confession and unable to imagine what a tumultuous and difficult childhood she must have had. He'd lost his parents, too, but at least he'd been lucky enough to have his brother, Cole, raising him and his sister, Joelle. They'd been a strong family unit—then and now. "How about relatives?"

She shook her head. "Both of my parents were only children, so I don't have any aunts and uncles, and my grandparents are dead, too."

He urged her to take a drink of her apple juice. "Do you remember how last night's accident happened?"

She paused, and he could see her straining to recall details. "I remember walking with you...but I was afraid of something?"

She looked at him with uncertainty in her pale blue gaze, waiting for him to confirm her question. "Yes, you were. What were you afraid of, sweetheart?"

She closed her eyes, and her face scrunched up in an obvious attempt to force thoughts into her head.

"I...I don't remember." Frustrated, she dropped her head back onto the pillow and released a low, discouraging growl. "How is it that I can recall so much about my past—you, even—but I can't remem-

ber other things? I feel like there's a huge, gaping
hole in my life.''

She sounded near to panic over her inability to control what her mind could and couldn't recollect.
Weaving their fingers together, he sought to soothe
her the best he could. ''I'm here for you, Natalie, for
anything you want or need. Anything at all.'' And he
meant it, too.

She pushed her breakfast tray aside, her appetite
obviously gone. ''I want my memory back. *All* of it,''
she said stubbornly.

Of course she'd ask for a wish he couldn't grant.
Knowing she was desperate, he focused on the positive. ''Tell you what, let's concentrate on the things
you *do* remember.''

Her gaze touched his eyes, lingering long enough
to make him feel as though she could see all the way
into his soul. She took in the rest of his features
slowly, as if scrutinizing each one, then finally came
to rest on his mouth.

''I remember kissing you,'' she said abruptly, her
voice low and husky with awareness. She dampened
her bottom lip with her tongue, and her breathing
deepened. ''Come here,'' she whispered.

Mesmerized by her request, he moved the small
table in front of her completely out of their way and
leaned toward her, bracing a hand on the pillow beside her head. The position caused his chest to press
against her full, generous breasts, and he had the fleeting thought that he wished they were both naked so
he could feel her skin on skin.

He was uncertain what she intended, but whatever she had planned, he was a willing participant.

Her soft, slender hand traveled up his arm to his shoulder, then her fingers slipped through the hair at the nape of his neck and she drew his head down to hers. Lost in the need reflecting in her eyes, he complied, watching as her lashes fluttered closed and her lips parted for him even before their mouths touched.

While their first kiss had been an act of desperation, this one was born of the sensuality that burned bright between them. She nibbled on his bottom lip, and he let her have free rein to taste and explore to her heart's content, no matter the cost to him physically. He was already hard and thick, completely aroused— a normal, lusty reaction when it came to her.

When she deepened the kiss, he welcomed the moist heat and slow, penetrating slide of her tongue, and met it with his own. He stroked long and slow, hot and deep, and she kissed him back the same way, eagerly and instinctively. So much passion. So much heat. Intense and uninhibited.

A purr of pleasure rumbled in her throat, and he groaned in appreciation, too. She was an irresistible temptation, a searing drug to his deprived libido, and she made him restless and hungry for more of her.

By the time she let him go, she was panting for breath and his own pulse was racing wildly. Their faces were still only inches away, and he wanted to drown in those trusting, velvety blue eyes of hers. Wanted to strip away the sheet and the flimsy gown separating them and make love to her.

The latter wasn't an option. Not here. Not now. Not until she regained her memory and could better define her emotions. It was obvious to him that she didn't realize that she'd been avoiding him and her attraction to him for months now. But *this* Natalie was giving into desires that had always been inside of her, desires she'd hidden from him before today.

Interesting.

A lazy smile hitched up the corner of his mouth. "And that was for…?" he murmured questioningly.

She caressed her palm along his cheek, skimmed her thumb along his full bottom lip, though her gaze never left his. "I needed to make sure what I feel for you is real."

"And is it?" He had to know.

"As real as I know it to be. You feel good and right, and I really like kissing you."

He laughed, relieved, and ran the tip of his finger down the slope of her cute nose. "Just so you know, you have permission to kiss me anytime you'd like."

Smiling, she settled back against her pillows, suddenly looking tired. While she might appear okay physically, he knew it would take a couple of days for her to fully regain her strength again. And right now, she needed more sleep.

He straightened, making a quick decision that would benefit them both. "I'm going to leave, but I'll be back in a little while."

Dread flared to life in her eyes. "Where are you going?"

Her panic-stricken expression clutched at him, and

he instantly tried to soothe her anxiety. "I need a
shower, shave and a change of clothes. And you need
to rest. Are you afraid to stay alone?" he asked
gently.

"Just a little nervous," she admitted, her cheeks
turning a pretty shade of pink. "I feel so out of place
and disoriented, and you're like an anchor in this
storm I seem to be caught up in."

"I'm sure that's very normal." Reaching for the
call button, he set it within her reach. "Tell you what,
here's the buzzer for the nurse, and if you need me
for anything at all, here are my cell phone and pager
numbers." He jotted both on a napkin and set it by
her phone. "Don't hesitate to call me, even if it's just
to hear my voice."

She inhaled deeply, as if inflating her courage.
"You must think I'm a complete basket case."

No, he didn't think that at all. Her nerves and fears
were legitimately based, but he wasn't about to enlighten her of that fact, or the reasons why. She didn't
need any more stress to deal with at the moment.

"I'm not always this clingy, am I?" she asked,
even as her lashes grew heavy and drooped.

She sounded so embarrassed at the thought that he
couldn't help but grin. "You're only clingy when it
counts, sweetheart," he teased.

"Good." Her eyes closed completely, and she
mumbled drowsily, "Will you bring me back fresh
clothes, too?"

She thought he could because she believed they
lived together. "You bet." Luckily for him he'd

claimed her car keys and ID from her purse before handing over her personal effects to the nurses, so he had everything he needed to get into her apartment and confiscate enough items to make it appear as though she'd moved into his house. But first, he had to call a cab to take him back to his car, which was still parked at Murphy's.

He remained by her bedside until her breathing grew deep and even in sleep before leaving her room. He stopped at the nurses' station, flashed his P.I. badge and gave them adamant orders that other than personnel, no one was to go into her room without someone calling and asking him first.

He wasn't taking any chances with her safety.

HANDS ON HIS HIPS, Noah glanced around what had once been *his* masculine bathroom, but now shared space with Natalie's feminine toiletries, and knew his cherished bachelorhood as he'd once known it was over—at least temporarily. The thought of trading in meaningless flings for a day-to-day intimacy with a woman didn't bother him as much as it should have, though—because it was Natalie, a woman he'd been chasing for so long. A woman who intrigued him and evoked the kind of emotions that, with other women, had sent him running in the other direction, but with her seemed so perfectly, inexplicably right.

At the moment, he refused to analyze his changing emotions, because he had a job to do and his feelings for Natalie couldn't get in the way of higher priorities, like keeping her safe and protected. Once she regained her memory and was no longer in danger, then they'd focus on *them.*

He headed back into his bedroom, made room in his closet for her stuff and finished putting away the clothes he'd taken from her apartment. While going through her belongings, he'd learned that she favored jeans and sweats, loose shirts and bulky sweaters. There wasn't a sexy outfit to be had in all of her attire, or the kind of clingy, flattering clothes most women with her kind of figure would have worn. It was as if she'd sought to hide her assets, rather than accentuate them.

That had been an interesting eye-opener, and he'd found the rest of her small studio apartment equally revealing. Instead of the warmth and intimacy he'd expected to find upon entering, the accommodations she called home had felt cold, empty and lonely. Her apartment was a compact place where she slept, ate meals and studied, as indicated by the pile of books stacked on a corner table near the only window in the room. There was nothing to indicate she led anything more than a quiet, solitary life.

The apartment had been filled with only the bare living necessities—a box spring and mattress in the combo bedroom-living room, along with a nightstand and dresser drawers that were old and scarred and didn't even match. Her small thirteen-inch TV sat on a plastic crate, and her small dining table was flanked by two old wooden chairs. Even her cupboards and refrigerator only held a few staple items.

He'd gotten the distinct impression that she could

get up and go at a moment's notice and not miss anything she left behind. There was nothing permanent to indicate she'd settled down for good in Oakland. Her belongings were meager, and he hadn't found anything to disclose who she was beyond what he already knew.

He'd even gone so far as to search drawers, hoping to find some kernel of information to help him better understand what had frightened her, but the only intriguing tidbit he'd discovered was an outdated woman's magazine she'd subscribed to with her name and a Reno, Nevada, address on the mailing label. He'd confiscated the item to help him find out about the life she'd led before moving to Northern California.

He emptied the final bag of clothes onto his bed to sort, and her intimate apparel tumbled out. He grinned as he picked up her underwear and rubbed the smooth fabric between his fingers, then inhaled the clean, powdery scent of fabric softener. He'd been surprised to find that she favored simple cotton panties when she had a body made for "barely there" lingerie, but she'd allowed a hint of femininity in the strip of lace around the waistband. Her bras were sheer, but plain, a thin, unadorned covering for her beautiful breasts.

There was nothing overtly sexy about any of her undergarments, and he'd no doubt seen racier, more provocative stuff in his years, but there was something about her no-frill approach that did it for him in a major way, if the raging hard-on straining against his jeans was any indication. Natalie was all woman, and she didn't need silk and lace to emphasize her attributes.

She was also a woman with deeply buried secrets, and he planned to discover what she'd been hiding.

Stuffing her panties and bras into a drawer he'd cleared for her, he also mixed a few articles of her clothing into his hamper just for good measure. Her college textbooks were now on his kitchen table, and he'd set the three music CDs he'd found at her place on top of his stereo cabinet.

Satisfied that his two-story house looked as though a woman lived there as well, Noah took a quick shower, shaved and made a quick call to Bobby and Cole to update them on Natalie's status and to remind them to play along with his cover of being her fiancé for the time being. He returned to the hospital with a fresh pair of her sweats, socks, underwear and her well-worn Keds to change into.

When he entered her room, she was up and talking to the doctor, and when she saw him, she graced him with a smile that quickened his pulse and made him feel like a teenager with a bad case of infatuation.

"Hi," she said, and motioned him over to her bed, her expression reflecting excitement. Once he was there, she grabbed his hand and gave it a squeeze. "Good news. The doctor is going to release me today."

He noticed that the IV had been taken off, and she was no longer hooked to the other monitors in the room. "That's great."

The doctor jotted a note on her chart, then glanced

at Noah pointedly. "She needs to take it easy for the next few days and get plenty of rest."

"Not a problem." He set her clothes on the side table, right next to a huge floral bouquet that must have arrived in his absence, then grinned down at Natalie. "I'll make sure she gets all the TLC she needs."

"Very good, then." The older man nodded his approval and slipped his pen back into his lab coat pocket. "She can change and get ready to leave, and I'll have the nurse bring in her personal items from last night."

The doctor exited the room, and Noah returned his attention to the gorgeous floral arrangement scenting the room, curious to know who had sent them. "Nice flowers," he commented, hoping his voice didn't reveal the tinge of jealousy he felt. Hoping, too, that she'd reveal their origin.

"Yes, they are beautiful." She reached out and fingered a pink rose petal, then met his gaze, her features softening with adoration. "Thank you for sending them. That was incredibly sweet of you, and the sentiment was very reassuring."

He swallowed not only his surprise, but the words of denial that immediately sprang to his lips. Whatever sentiment was written on the card attached to the bouquet had given her the impression that he'd bought the flowers for her, and his fingers itched to pluck the envelope from the center of the arrangement and read the attached note for himself.

Schooling his expression and summoning restraint

and a grin, he played along with the scenario. "You're welcome."

With a long, lingering sigh, she sat up in bed and carefully swung her legs over the side of the mattress. "Well, I guess I'd better get dressed so you can spring me from this joint."

He helped her stand with his hand encircling her arm, waited to make sure she was steady on her feet, then handed her the clothes he'd brought for her. He watched as she headed toward the small bathroom, and nearly groaned at the sweet, delectable view he caught sight of.

Trying to preserve a bit of modesty, one of her hands clutched at the open folds at the back of her hospital gown to hold them closed. While she did a decent job of covering herself, he was still treated to tantalizing glimpses of the rounded curves of her buttocks that gave way to her slender, smooth thighs.

Once she disappeared behind the closed door, he inhaled a deep, steady breath that did little to ease the tightening in his groin, and focused his attention back on the floral arrangement. Knowing he only had minutes before Natalie returned, he removed the envelope, withdrew the florist card within and read the note someone had written specifically for her.

You'll always be mine.

Brief and succinct, that's all the inscription said, with no name or signature to go with the very personal, possessive comment. Unease prickled through Noah, along with a healthy dose of fury that someone would prey upon Natalie so brazenly. And just how far was this crazed lunatic willing to go to stalk her?

The answer to his own question upped his inner rage a few notches and instigated another fierce surge of protectiveness toward Natalie.

Thank God she believed that he'd sent the flowers, and he didn't intend to correct her assumption. He supposed in her frame of mind she'd taken the remark to mean that Noah still considered her *his,* despite the accident and amnesia. She'd taken the note as a reassurance, and had no idea just how threatening those words were.

Whoever had been following her last night knew that she was in this hospital and was keeping tabs on her, which was a scary prospect. Noah was grateful that patient information was privileged and wasn't given out to just anyone, because Natalie's amnesia was something someone with sinister intent would no doubt use to his advantage.

Finding a notepad in the side drawer, Noah ripped off a page and quickly scribbled the name, address and phone number of the florist shop printed on the outside of the envelope, then slipped the paper into his pocket. Another piece of evidence he planned to follow up on later. He hoped he'd be able to learn the identity of the sender through the shop and hunt him down from there.

If this creep wanted to play cat and mouse with Natalie, then Noah would be the Doberman pinscher in the scenario, because he was determined to catch this guy before he caught Natalie.

SITTING ACROSS FROM NOAH in a small, cozy kitchen nook, Natalie reached for her second slice of pepperoni-and-cheese pizza, still absorbing the fact that she and Noah lived together in his two-story house.

So far she'd only seen the lower level of the structure, and she had to admit not only to herself, but to Noah as well, that nothing looked familiar. Not the tweed sofa and big-screen TV in the living room, nor the kitchen where she was certain they'd eaten many meals together. She'd racked her brain for a niggle of recognition, and hadn't been aware of the distressed sound that had escaped her until Noah had gathered her in his strong arms and told her to be patient and give it time.

His closeness, warmth and arousing male scene was all it took to soothe her frazzled nerves. She'd clung to him because he made her feel safe and secure, and as though she belonged in his embrace. In his life. From there, she'd relaxed and told herself to enjoy the man so willing to cater to her every whim and desire. A man who inspired decadent fantasies and a hunger that had nothing to do with the food she was feasting on.

Natalie took a bite of her pizza and moaned her appreciation of the delicious, savory taste filling her mouth. True to his word, Noah had ordered a large pizza for her as soon as they'd arrived at his house, and compared to the bland breakfast and lunch she'd been served at the hospital, the delicacy was like ambrosia to her taste buds and she couldn't seem to get enough.

Noah grinned at her as he washed down a bite of

his own pizza with a drink from his bottle of cold beer. "I take it your stomach is happy?"

Surprisingly, *she* felt happy, despite every reason she had to feel uncertain. "Very," she said, and darted her tongue out to catch a string of cheese from the corner of her mouth. His dark, lazy gaze watched the slow slide of her tongue, setting off a fluttering sensation in the pit of her belly. "The flavor is *better* than I remember."

He chuckled, a low, pleasant rumbling sound. "You're very easy to please."

Before she could stop herself, she slanted him a flirtatious glance and asked seductively, "Am I?"

Slowly, he licked smears of sauce from his fingers in long, slow laps she felt in intimate places. "Yeah, you are." Sexual connotation deepened his sexy voice, and a naughty twinkle glimmered in his eyes.

A smoldering heat flared through her, a sensation she didn't bother to fight. "You're a tease."

The corner of his mouth hitched with a wicked grin, and a sable brow lifted with amusement. "You started this, sweetheart, not me."

Unable to argue, she ducked her head and brought up an issue on her mind. "Noah, I've been meaning to ask…since we're engaged, how come I don't have a ring?" It seemed like such a forward question, but one that had become necessary in order for her to fill in more blank memories. "Or is it with my personal belongings from the hospital?"

He shook his head and took a long drink of his

beer before answering. "No, you don't have an engagement ring. We'd talked about going to pick one out together, but that was before the accident."

She smiled, accepting his answer without questioning him further because it made so much sense, and they finished their dinner with a keen awareness swirling in the air between them. The more she was around Noah, the more she wanted him, with an intensity that kept growing stronger, more insistent. And if she couldn't remember being with him intimately, then she wanted new memories to replace the ones she'd lost. That much she knew for certain.

Standing, Noah tossed their empty paper plates into the trash and cleared the table, putting the leftover pizza into the refrigerator. He came back with a glass of water and two white pills.

"Here's some Motrin to help keep your headache away." He gently brushed a finger across her cheek, then urged her to take the medication. Once she'd swallowed both tablets, he asked, "Can I get you anything else?"

A loaded question, and one she handled with restraint. "I'd love a long, hot bath."

He swept into a gallant bow that made her smile. "Your wish is my command."

As she stared up into his gorgeous face, she wondered if she requested her true heart's desire at the moment if he'd obey and take her right there in the kitchen. On the table, on the floor, up against the wall, she didn't care, just so long as she felt his need for her in return. The naughty, scintillating thought tantalized her, teased her, caused a pulsing knot of anticipation to pull tight in her stomach, and lower.

He grabbed her hand, led her upstairs, and she followed him into a large, spacious room decorated in blue-and-beige tones and furnished in dark oak. A king-size bed dominated the area, covered by a soft, rumpled comforter in a masculine design. She tried to remember making love to Noah there. While she couldn't recall specific memories, her mind had no problem conjuring images of their naked limbs entwined and Noah's strong body moving over hers, filling her, thrusting hard and deep as she arched beneath him.

The mental imagine was so realistic her womb contracted, her panties grew damp, and much to her chagrin a whimpering sound caught in her throat.

Noah glanced at her, concerned. "Hey, you okay?"

If he only knew the truth...that around him she couldn't get sex off her mind. Had this man always had such an instantaneous effect on her libido? If so, she was in big, big trouble because she didn't know how long she could resist the urge to give in to the provocative fantasy that had just filtered through her head.

"I'm fine." Her voice was husky.

"Okay." He stared at her a moment longer through narrowed eyes, as if to make sure she was truly stable. "Go ahead and get yourself something to sleep in, and I'll run you a hot bath." He slipped through an adjoining door, leaving her alone. Seconds later she heard the rush of running water.

She released a deep breath that did little to ease the throbbing ache in intimate places. No, she didn't think anything would be able to relieve that shameless, reckless longing except for Noah's touch.

Feeling a bit lost, and not certain where to start her search, she began opening dresser drawers. The first one was filled with his socks and briefs, the second with his white undershirts. Peeking from beneath the cotton shirts was a glint of steel, and upon closer inspection she was shocked to find a gun in a leather holster. She frowned, wondering why he had such a lethal weapon stashed in his drawer.

"Is something wrong, Natalie?"

She jumped at the sound of his voice, so close. She'd been so absorbed by the revolver that she hadn't heard him come up beside her. She looked up at him. "You have a gun?"

"I'm a P.I., sweetheart," he said simply, gently. "Owning a gun is part of the job."

A very logical explanation. She shook her head. "Of course. I just don't remember you carrying one." The story of her life, lately. She wondered if she'd ever get used to the various voids in her memory.

"I wear it pretty much on a daily basis, and I took it off when we got home. But right now it's not loaded, though the clip is right there beside it." He shut the drawer and opened the one below it. "Your stuff is right here."

"Thank you." She pulled out a fresh pair of undies, hopelessly frustrated that he knew right where

her things were located while she was floundering just
to find her panties.

Walking over to the closet, he grabbed a long cotton chemise. "And here's your nightgown."

"Are you sure I don't wear one of your shirts to
bed?" It wasn't so much a question as it was a hidden
request. She wanted to feel as close as possible to
him, even while sleeping. A security blanket of sorts,
no matter how silly it seemed.

He stopped in his tracks, her cotton gown fisted in
his hand, his entire body tense. "Would you like to?"

He'd answered her question with one of his own,
which didn't tell her what she wanted to know. Hell,
maybe she slept in the nude and he was just trying to
preserve her modesty until she felt better.

It wasn't necessary. "I'd love to sleep in one of
your shirts, as long as you don't mind."

"Not at all." Back at the dresser, he withdrew an
extra-large white T-shirt and gave it to her, his movements quick and efficient. He disappeared back into
the bathroom, turned off the water and returned seconds later. "The tub is full and waiting for you. Can
you handle things from here, or do you need help?"

Oh, she was sorely tempted to tell him she needed
his assistance, just because she wanted to feel his
hands on her naked flesh as he undressed her. And
she certainly wouldn't mind having him scrub her
back or wash the rest of her body while he was at it.
She shivered at the sensual thought.

But while he seemed concerned for her welfare,
there was a sudden reserve about him that puzzled

her, and she didn't push the issue. "Don't worry about me, Noah. I'll be fine."

"Leave the door open," he said, grabbing a pair of gray cotton sweatpants for himself. "I'll be downstairs in my office, so just call me if you need anything."

And then he was gone, making her wonder why he didn't change in front of her if they lived together. Shrugging her shoulders and refusing to let such an inconsequential thought hurt her already tired brain, she stepped into the bathroom. She was greeted by a fragrant cloud of steam and a large tub brimming with water and bubbles. She spotted her floral body wash beside the tub, knowing that Noah had thoughtfully added it to the water.

After stripping off her clothes, she rummaged through the drawers, recognizing her stuff and finding a scrunchie for her hair. She rubbed a spot clean on the fogged mirror and proceeded to pull the shoulder-length strands into a ponytail so they wouldn't get wet.

She caught sight of her reflection in the mirror, drawing her gaze to the lush curves of her body. Absently, she cupped her large breasts in her palms and grazed her fingers over the tips. She shivered as her nipples puckered and tingled. Closing her eyes, she touched elsewhere, skimming her hands over intimate dips and hollows.

She imagined it was Noah caressing her, and her heart thumped hard in her chest as her body came vibrantly alive, as if something deep inside of her was gradually awakening, demanding attention and release. Her skin grew damp from the moisture in the bathroom and her own arousal, her nerves strung tight, and the provocative sensations grew stronger with every slick slide of her hands, along with a carnal craving that stole her breath.

She felt sexual and sensual, her response wrapped up in illicit fantasies of Noah. He was the only connection she had to the past and present and the burning, aching need consuming her. She needed him in ways even she didn't understand, but she trusted him, with her body and even her lost soul. And while there were still so many gaps in her mind, there was one thing she knew for certain.

The erotic hunger within her wouldn't be denied much longer.

4

NOAH YANKED OFF his clothes, flung them onto the small leather couch in his downstairs office and pulled on his cotton sweatpants, forgoing a shirt as he always did at night. Sitting behind his desk, he picked up the piece of paper with the florist's name and phone number he'd jotted down at the hospital earlier, intent on focusing his restless energy on business.

Instead, sinful, brazen thoughts ruthlessly intruded, of Natalie upstairs in the bathtub, naked and wet, her skin soft, sleek and fragrant. The vivid mental image of touching all that feminine flesh with his hands and tasting it with slow, leisurely licks of his tongue gave him a thick, rampant hard-on, which was becoming a too frequent occurrence when it came to her. One that was getting more and more difficult to control.

He shifted in his seat, which did nothing to help ease his throbbing discomfort. He groaned and scrubbed a hand along his taut jaw. Being chivalrous was killing him in excruciatingly slow degrees, and Natalie wasn't helping matters by sending out tempting sexual vibes that were doing a damn good job of weakening his resolve.

Her uninhibited behavior was understandable in her

amnesiac state because she had no clear recollection of her reserved response to him before the accident. Yet he found it hard to reconcile the trusting, sensual creature she was now with the self-contained woman she'd been around him before the accident. The two were complete opposites, but both were enigmas with secrets he wanted to unearth and explore.

He suspected her current open mind-set had a lot to do with the fact that she believed they were engaged and living together. That sense of security gave her more freedom to be affectionate and flirtatious, daring even. It was a playful side to her that he enjoyed, yet the contrast made him even more curious as to what had kept her so reserved and private before the accident. What had been so devastating that she'd kept herself at arm's length and lived such a solitary life? Obviously, it had something to do with the haunting fear he'd witnessed right before and after she'd kissed him in that dark shop alcove.

He had every intention of discovering the answer to that particular question. Her past obviously affected the present and her future…as well as any chance he might have with her. But along with his determination to make sense of the mystery she'd become, he couldn't help but wonder, and worry, that once her memories returned, would she retreat from him yet again?

The possibility made his gut twist. He knew his time with her was limited, and that meant using their current predicament to cement an emotional bond between them that would last beyond finding the guy who was stalking her. And during their time together he had to resist her newfound femininity and sexy overtures. He wasn't about to take advantage of her mind's current inability to remember their prior platonic relationship.

His still-hard erection mocked him. He was a man with a healthy sexual drive, and he'd been celibate too long because he hadn't wanted any other woman except for Natalie for months now. Having her in his house, in his bed, was going to be pure torture.

With a harsh breath, he cleared his mind of his sorry aroused state and reached for the phone. He dialed Bobby's cell phone number, and his friend answered on the second ring.

"Malone here," he said, his tone curt and businesslike.

"Hey, it's Noah. I need to ask a favor."

"You got it." Bobby's reply was automatic. As good friends who worked in the same investigative field, they often traded professional favors. "What's up?"

"I need you to do a check on something for me." Leaning back in his chair, Noah explained about the bouquet of flowers that had been delivered to Natalie at the hospital and the ominous note attached. "Could you stop at the florist shop, flash your badge and find out who sent the arrangement? I want a name and address and a credit card number if the perp used one."

"Consider it done. In fact, I was just heading out

to get a bite to eat and I'll swing by the florist afterward.''

''Great.'' Noah gave him the address of the place. ''I'd do it myself, but I don't want to leave Natalie alone.'' And he obviously didn't want her going with him, since she believed he'd been the one to send the arrangement.

''By the way, how is she doing?'' Bobby asked.

''Pretty good. She's accepted the situation, which makes things easier for me.''

Bobby chuckled. ''As opposed to *harder?*'' he joked.

Noah winced at Bobby's well-aimed innuendo. His friend knew him too well. ''Call me when you have the information, wise guy.'' He hung up the phone before Bobby could give him any more flack.

He glanced at the clock—thirty minutes had passed since he'd left Natalie upstairs. Figuring he'd check on her before Bobby called back, he headed up to his room. She hadn't completely shut the bathroom door, and he didn't care for the silence that greeted him.

Slowly, he pushed open the door. ''Natalie?'' he called softly, not wanting to frighten her but concerned about her not responding.

No answer, so he stepped inside, his gaze immediately drawn to the woman who'd fallen asleep in his tub. She was submerged to her neck, her head resting against the rim, and there were just enough bubbles to keep her decently covered—and to preserve his sanity. Thank God.

He hunkered down next to the tub and gently

skimmed his fingers over her warm, flushed cheek. "Natalie, honey, wake up."

Her lashes fluttered open, and she smiled up at him drowsily. "I fell asleep," she murmured.

"You most certainly did." Standing, he grabbed the big fluffy towel hanging over the brass rod so he could leave it within reaching distance for her before he bolted back out of the bathroom. "You need to get out of the tub, get dressed and into bed."

Just as he turned back around to face her she stood up, without wearing an ounce of timidity, or anything else for that matter. His breath left his lungs painfully and the last bit of his fortitude fled as he stared in awed fascination at the rivulets of water sluicing down her centerfold body.

Mouth dry, his avid gaze followed the sleek trail of moisture, taking in her plump, full breasts tipped with dusky pink areolas and nipples as hard as pebbles that all but begged for him to nibble, lick and suck. He was certain he could span her tiny waist with his big hands, and she had the sexiest navel he'd ever seen. The dewy thatch of honey-blond curls between her thighs teased his imagination of what lay beyond, and those endlessly long legs of hers were made to bring a man to his knees and tempt him to sin.

He was the furthest thing to a saint when it came to her, and his shaft twitched, throbbed and swelled full to bursting. She was every hot, lascivious scenario he'd ever envisioned. Every carnal thought that had passed through his mind. Every erotic daydream he'd ever had.

And reality, in all its breathtaking glory, beckoned....

"Noah?" She shivered, and goose bumps dotted her smooth, wet flesh. "You're looking at me as if you've never seen me naked before."

Oh, hell. Shaking himself out of his lustful stupor, he summoned a playful grin. "Honey, that's just the kind of effect you have on me." That much was the truth.

Her fingers fluttered along her belly, and her breasts quivered at the brief, absentminded touch. "You have that kind of effect on me, too, and you're not even naked."

He swallowed a groan. Resigned to remaining in the bathroom with her, he kept his eyes safely above her shoulders and opened the towel for her. "Step out of the tub so we can get you dried off."

She did as he requested, and he briskly swiped her dry from neck to toes, ignoring her pleasurable moans while reciting multiplication tables in his mind to keep himself distracted from the task at hand. Finding the shirt he'd given her earlier, he yanked it over her head and waited for her to push her arms through the sleeves, then handed over her panties for her to slip into.

Once she was decently covered and she'd unclipped her hair, he led her back into the adjoining room. His movements were quick, efficient and economical, with no room for anything sexual to intervene. He pulled down the covers on the bed, patted the cool sheet, and she obediently crawled up onto the mattress.

Despite the magnitude of his longing for her, his actions were as honorable as the oath he'd made to protect and serve his country when he'd joined the marines. He pulled the covers up to her chest, and just when he thought he was in the clear and would escape the room without further incident, Natalie wrapped her arms around his neck and looked up at him with a sultry invitation in her gaze.

She drew his head down and skimmed her lips along the corner of his mouth and across his cheek, her breath warm and sweet. "Come to bed with me," she whispered.

Every cell in his body screamed *yes*. Heat flashed through him, making him ache with raw desire, and he clutched the bedspread in his fists to keep him grounded, physically and mentally. He knew without a doubt she didn't have sleeping on her mind, and he also knew he was precariously close to giving in to what they both wanted so badly. It would be so, so easy to crawl under the covers with her and sink deep into her willing body. To lose himself in her heat and softness, and finally quench the feverish hunger burning inside him.

He couldn't be so selfish with his needs, not when there was so much more at stake—foremost the risk of her regretting their lovemaking once she regained her memory. With his hormones rallying in protest of his decision, he strove to let her down gently, in a way she wouldn't construe as an outright rejection.

"I'm expecting a call from Bobby." Unwinding her arms from his neck, he placed a kiss in each of her palms. "You get some rest and I'll be back up in a little while, okay?"

An adorable pout puffed out her bottom lip, but she issued no argument, just sought for a kernel of reassurance. "Promise?"

He nodded, unable to refuse her simple request. "Yeah, I promise," he said, sealing his own fate when he'd originally intended to crash on the couch downstairs for the night.

Satisfied that he'd return later, she snuggled deeper beneath the blankets, sighed and let her lashes drift shut.

Unplugging the phone in the room so Bobby's call wouldn't disturb her, Noah went back to his office, knowing it would be hours until he joined Natalie in his bed. He wanted her deep asleep and unaware of him before he dared to slip under the covers with her.

Ten minutes later Bobby called back with the information Noah was waiting for.

"This guy isn't stupid," Bobby said, a thread of disgust in his voice. "He paid cash for the flowers and gave the cashier what I highly suspect is a bogus name and an address that isn't his."

Surprised, Noah asked, "You ran a check already?"

"Yep, and you're not going to like what I'm about to tell you."

Feeling distinctly uneasy, he stabbed his fingers through his already mussed hair. "Give it to me straight, Malone." The request was unnecessary. Bobby wasn't one to bullshit around with something so serious.

"The guy who placed the order used the name Richard Haynes, who just happens to be a prominent surgeon in San Francisco who is squeaky clean, so I'm fairly certain that isn't the perp's real name, though I'll follow up on that tomorrow." He paused for a moment, then revealed, "And the contact address he used on the form came up as none other than Natalie's apartment."

Noah's stomach cramped as though he'd been sucker-punched. "He used *her* address?" he asked incredulously.

"Appears so. How's that for being ballsy?"

Noah rubbed his fingers across his forehead. "It's goddamn unbelievable."

The guy, whoever he was, knew where Natalie lived. The knowledge stunned and infuriated Noah, and while he hated the helpless feeling of not knowing the true identity of the stalker, he was grateful that she was safe with him at his house.

"Thanks for the info, Bobby," he said, grateful, too, for his friend's connections and support. "I owe you one."

"Buy me a beer once all this blows over and we'll call it even. In the meantime, watch your back. And Natalie's."

"I plan to." He hung up the phone, and turned his attention to the Reno, Nevada, address he'd confiscated from Natalie's place earlier that day.

He booted up his computer, jumped on the Internet and did an extensive search on an online database and a private network he belonged to that narrowed down her old address to an apartment complex. He scribbled down the manager's name and phone number to call on Monday, then spent the next few hours making notes on the various sources he wanted to contact to get a lead on her background, as well as information on the kind of life she led in Reno—where she worked, who she dated and what had prompted her to move.

It was after midnight when he finally dragged himself back upstairs to his bedroom. He slipped into the darkened room quietly, squinting to see his way to the opposite side of the bed where Natalie had fallen asleep. He felt his blood chill when he realized the covers were thrown back and the bed was empty. The light in the bathroom wasn't on, either, and a dozen unpleasant scenarios flew through his head before he could stop them.

There was a movement by the window, a flash of white that captured his attention. His muscles tensed, ready for action, his mind already contemplating the short distance to his gun tucked away in his dresser.

"Noah?"

Natalie's soft, husky voice reached him just as she stepped out of the shadows by the window and came into better focus. He relaxed a fraction, bewitched by the moonlight streaming into the room that silhouetted her body beneath his white T-shirt. Her blond hair was tousled around her shoulders, and a silvery, shimmering light haloed her head. She looked ethereal, and too damned sexy for his peace of mind.

He cleared his throat and stepped deeper into the room. "Yeah, it's me. Are you okay?"

Her shoulders lifted in a shrug. "As good as can be expected, I suppose. I was just going to come looking for you."

"You should be in bed." Stopping in front of her, he narrowed his gaze to better take in her features, wondering if she was in any pain. "Do you need another Motrin for your muscle aches and your head?"

"No, I'm fine physically." A small smile touched her lips and her eyes shone with uncertainty. "It's the mental stuff that keeps throwing me for a loop."

He gently rubbed his hands up and down her arms, warming her skin, causing his own to tighten in response to touching her. "Give it time," he said softly. "You're not going to regain your memory overnight."

Her brows puckered in frustration. "I know that, but when I try to sleep, my dreams are fragmented and confusing, and there's so much I don't understand. I see shadows and I feel like I'm running from something or someone, but I can't grasp what the threat is, or if it's even real."

Her voice quivered, and he suspected her subconscious was trying to break through with the truth. Her big blue eyes stared up at him as if he held the answers to her secrets and the key to all her hidden depths. He wished he did, but he was learning about her past right along with her.

"I know it's difficult, but the doctor said not to force yourself to remember, because that can possibly suppress your memories deeper."

"I can't help it." Moisture glittered in her eyes, and her voice caught with emotion. "I feel so lost, and there's only one thing I'm sure of at this moment."

"And what's that?"

Her gaze held his, the vulnerability etching her expression so heartbreakingly real. "My desire for you." Stepping closer, she placed her hands on his bare chest and rubbed her soft, cool palms over his hot flesh. "What I feel for you is so intense and overwhelming, and I know you're trying to be a gentleman because of the accident, but right now I *crave* you, Noah Sommers. I need to feel alive, and I don't think I could bear it if you turned me down right now."

In a move that stunned him, she peeled the shirt she wore over her head and dropped it to the floor. Sliding her arms around his neck before he could back away, she aligned their bodies from chest to thighs, and nuzzled her lips against his throat. "Make love to me, Noah," she whispered huskily.

The blood in Noah's veins sizzled and his shaft thickened against her belly through his sweatpants. Her full, naked breasts and all her smooth bare skin seared him, wreaking havoc with his conscience and personal ethics. He fought his own weakness, but in the end he didn't have it in him to say no to her sensual plea, not when she needed this physical connection in a way that superceded mere sex. He could give her the intimacy her body and soul yearned for, even knowing he'd be sacrificing his own pleasure for hers.

Without a word, he led her back to the bed, pressed her down onto the mattress and positioned himself so that he was half on top of her. With his chest pinned against her lush breasts, he wedged his knee between her thighs and pushed his fingers through her hair, capturing her lips in a hungry, greedy kiss.

She opened to him with a sigh of abandon, welcoming the thrust of his tongue deep inside and meeting it with her own. Ready and willing. Wild and wanton. It was a kiss as seductive as the night, as electrifying as the attraction they'd resisted for too long.

With his free hand, he began a slow, tentative exploration, seeking erogenous zones and all those sensitive feminine places women loved to be stroked and caressed. He trailed his fingers along the silky skin of her neck and shoulders and felt her shiver in response. His hand skimmed lower, until he finally cupped a smooth, firm breast in his palm. He kneaded that generous swell of flesh he'd admired for months now, savored the exquisite feel of her, then rasped his thumb across the pearled tips of her nipples.

She moaned low and deep, and grasping his hair in her fists, she tugged his head down. Knowing instinctively what she wanted, he obeyed her silent command and buried his face between the soft fullness of her breasts. His teeth scraped over one perfect swell, followed by the slow, wet, luxurious lap of his tongue all the way to the burgeoning crest. She gasped in delight, her fingers biting into the muscles of his upper arms as she arched her back, silently begging him for more.

Opening his mouth wide, he suckled her hard and deep, and laved her nipple with the flat of his tongue. Sliding his hand along the curve of her waist and around to her bottom, he filled his palm with one delectable cheek. He squeezed gently, then slid his fingers to the crease of her knee, pulled her leg over his hip, and rocked slowly, rhythmically against her.

Their position was as intimate as making love, his shaft hot and heavy against the juncture of her thighs. Yet judging by her restless movements and the anxious, needy sounds she made deep in her throat, it wasn't enough. She was on fire, desperate for release, and he sought to give it to her in the most erotic, carnal way possible—for his own pleasure as much as her own.

Moving quickly, fluidly, he sat up and knelt between her sprawled legs. He looked up the length of her gorgeous body to her face, searching for any signs of apprehension, and found nothing but passion and need. The trust she offered him with her body was humbling. She lay there, seductive as sin itself, her lashes half mast, her lips moist and parted, and her white cotton panties drenched with desire. For him. His nostrils flared as he inhaled her heady, arousing scent. He felt huge, hot and throbbing, and he feared he'd come just by looking at her.

"Touch me, Noah," she said, her voice a low, caressing sound that made him a willing slave to her every desire. *"Please."*

Needing a moment to regroup and calm his own racing heart, he lightly strummed his fingers along her flesh through her damp panties, and stopped when he felt her tremble in response. "With my fingers?"

Her breathing deepened, and she nodded. "Yes…"

Grasping the back of her knee, he leaned down and placed hot, damp kisses all the way up her thigh, and stopped short of his ultimate goal. "How about with my mouth?" he said, breathing hot, moist air on her skin.

She squirmed and clutched the sheets in her hands. "Oh, *yes.*"

"What about my tongue?" Moving a bit higher, he delved the tip of his tongue into her navel in lazy, sensuous swirls that made her moan and thrash. "Do you want me to use that, too?"

"Oh, yes…" An impatient sob escaped her. "Noah, stop teasing me, *please.*"

Knowing he'd tormented her enough, he pulled her panties down her long legs and off, tossed them to the floor, and slid his palms back up the insides of her slender thighs until his thumbs finally grazed the outer folds of her feminine flesh. He looked his fill of her, so plump and pink and glistening. And so uninhibited he knew she'd allow him *anything* at all.

It was a heady, dizzying thought. He raised his gaze to her face, taking in her flushed cheeks and those unwavering blue eyes waiting for him to make her feel alive, and cherished, and desired. It was a simple task from his perspective, and he separated the slick folds of her sex with his fingers and stroked her slowly, seductively. A deep, throaty, on-the-edge moan escaped her, and her body undulated for a more explicit touch.

Done toying with her, he settled himself between her spread thighs, slid his hands beneath her hips, and pressed an intimate, openmouthed kiss at the very heart of her. He nibbled her delicate flesh and gently suckled her swollen clitoris while his fingers continued to explore. She was incredibly sweet and tender, so open and responsive, he knew he'd never get enough of her.

At the first heated, silken swirl of his tongue, her entire body bowed and trembled on the precipice of an orgasm. With the second and third strokes she came with a gut-wrenching and very vocal climax that rippled through him, as well. He ruthlessly took her over the edge, reveling in her satisfaction, in the ecstasy he alone had given her.

While she floated back down from her release, he leisurely kissed his way back up the length of her, drinking in her pale, moonlit flesh and the tiny quivers still reverberating through her body. Her breathing was erratic, and she slid her fingers into his hair, holding him close as he tugged at a nipple with his lips and rolled the straining bead against his tongue before moving up to nuzzle her neck.

He'd thought he'd given her enough pleasure to exhaust her for the night—hell, *he* was drained and he hadn't had the luxury of coming—yet the provocative, restless way she tried to move over him made him quickly realize that one climax had seemingly only whet her appetite for more.

Her mouth landed on his chest, and her teeth scraped across his nipple, distracting him as her palm slipped down his abdomen and beneath the waistband of his sweatpants. In an aggressive move he hadn't anticipated, she took his hot, rigid penis in her hand and encircled him in a slow, squeezing stroke that made his entire body shake.

His hips bucked instinctively, and a low, guttural groan hissed out between his clenched teeth. Heeding the warning of his own impending orgasm rushing forth, he grabbed her wrist and pulled her fingers away, determined to regain the upper hand with her and the situation.

She looked up with him, her eyes fever-bright and her features just as wild and untamed. "Noah," she whimpered, the sound needy and utterly demanding. She twisted and strained toward him, rubbing her sweet curves against his chest, belly and thighs.

He stretched her arms above her head to maintain control, and held her wrists together with one hand. "Shh, baby," he murmured soothingly in her ear. "I'll give you whatever you need."

"I need *you*," she said raggedly. "Inside me."

He closed his eyes and inhaled deeply. Her carnal request seared his senses and came damn close to crippling his fortitude. With a strength that nearly killed him, he said, "I don't have any condoms to

make love to you. Not that way." They were the
hardest words he'd ever spoken, considering he knew
he had a few packets in the bathroom's medicine cabinet.

A desperate sound filled the darkened room, and
she writhed against his hold. "*Please,* Noah."

"Don't worry, I'll take care of you." He cursed
himself for being such a gentleman when he ached to
drive deep inside of her and assuage his own raging
lust. Then he dipped his head to slide his tongue along
her lower lip. "Just relax and stop fighting me."

His mouth came down on hers, hot and hard, and
the seduction started all over again. While the first
time had been a slow, easy buildup, Noah skipped all
coaxing preliminaries and opted for a single-minded
approach to assuaging her sexual energy.

His free hand slipped between her thighs, and he
finessed her with sleek caresses before slipping one
finger, then two, deep inside of her. He delved his
thumb against her softly swollen flesh, and she
groaned and tried to tug her arms free, but he refused
to let her go. He kissed her rapaciously, making love
to her not only with his mouth but his hand, as well.
His fingers thrust into her in a slow, thick rhythm,
and his thumb added to the friction.

He felt her inner muscles contract around his fingers and knew she was on the verge of another orgasm. He lifted his mouth from hers just as she
reached the peak, because this time he wanted to
watch her as she came for him. Her legs clamped tight

around his hand, and her hips surged upward, seeking and taking what he offered.

Her eyes fluttered closed and her head rolled back on the pillow as her body convulsed with a hard, all-consuming release that made her shudder and scream. He didn't stop after the first wave, but ruthlessly pushed her higher, wringing every last bit of tension from her with yet another slow, sinuous orgasm that left her limp and sated. As he gradually brought her back down with tender caresses and soft kisses, she wept his name, and it was the sweetest sound he'd ever heard.

He released her hands, and she opened her eyes and glanced up at him with a dreamy smile that told him he'd satisfied her plenty…for tonight, anyway. The woman was utterly insatiable, as though it had been years since she'd allowed herself such sexual freedom and she was making up for lost time.

With a soft, repleted sigh, she snuggled up to his side. Wrapping an arm over his belly, she rested her head on his shoulder and promptly fell asleep, leaving him reeling from the entire episode…and battling with the fiercest erection of his entire life.

He thought about heading to the bathroom to give his body some badly needed relief from the throbbing pressure, but Natalie was draped over him and he didn't want to disturb her or, Lord forbid, wake her up and have the lascivious cycle start all over again. He'd never survive another round.

He inhaled a calming breath and willed himself to relax and focus on what lay ahead for him and Natalie—mainly, to discover the key to her past and the threat looming over her. There was still so much he didn't know about her, so much he didn't understand. Despite all that, there was one thing he knew for absolute certain. He cared for Natalie, and that knowledge shook him up in a way nothing ever had.

The feelings crowding his chest had been completely foreign to him until Natalie. He was falling hard and fast for her, rushing headlong into emotions he'd never before allowed with a woman. He'd always been the one to pull back in a relationship, to withhold, because it was easier and smarter to keep his distance than to get sentimentally involved and get hurt.

Maintaining a light, flirtatious demeanor had come easily to him, and he was beginning to suspect he'd just never come across the right woman to inspire anything deeper, to make him want to take a leap beyond a superficial relationship and take a chance with his emotions.

Natalie, quite possibly, could be that woman. Because for the first time in his adult life he instinctively wanted to *give* to another person, as well as keep her safe from harm.

He'd never taken care of another person before, had never taken on such a huge responsibility as she presented—not in such a personal, soul-stirring way. Being the strong one in their family, the protector, had always been Cole's job—a huge obligation thrust upon him at such a young age, and one Cole had taken very seriously. It had allowed Noah to adopt a carefree facade that hid a deeper pain and an inner fear of getting too attached to any one person.

His parents' nasty divorce had shaken the foundation of his stable young life, and he'd spent years wondering why a mother who'd claimed to love her children hadn't fought for custody of her two oldest boys, but instead had chosen to rip Joelle from their lives as a way of hurting their father. Her selfish actions had not only pained Noah, but caused him to question what he'd done wrong to make his mother shun him.

In an attempt to make up for that feeling of inadequacy, he'd driven himself to please his father, a man with a heart of gold who made sure all his children knew his affection was unconditional. Noah had thrived on the security and stability of his dad's love, and had been so devastated by his death he still felt the loss.

And now fresh misgivings were rearing their ugly head, because he knew when everything was said and done with Natalie and she regained the memory of her old life, he stood to lose yet another person who'd affected him in such a profound way. A woman who made him realize just how empty and hollow his life had been without her in it.

The revelation caused his heart to thump hard in his chest. Turning his head, he buried his nose in her hair, breathing deeply and losing himself in her scent. He resigned himself to the fact that he had no choice but to take things one day at a time with her and hope that she didn't resent him when her memory returned. He also prayed that when that day of reckoning came, she'd understand that he'd used her genuine desire and trust as a way to protect her.

5

NOAH GROANED DEEP in his throat as soft, warm lips nestled against his neck, smooth hands caressed his chest, and long, slender limbs tangled around his legs. The dream filtering through his mind and arousing his body was so erotically intense, like his fondest, most carnal fantasy come to life. He fought the consciousness that beckoned, somehow knowing if he allowed himself to wake up, the provocative dream would dissipate, and he wanted to enjoy the inviting sensations rippling through him. Wanted to let the fantasy continue and see where it led.

His mind filled with images of Natalie, putting her in the starring role of temptress. A damp, ravishing mouth traveled lower, spreading sensuous kisses across his collarbone and down his chest to his nipples. A wet tongue stroked, laved, and he groaned as teeth scraped across the rigid tip.

Finely textured sweeps of her hair tickled his belly, heightening his need as her hot, moist breath sizzled across his skin, along with more luxurious, biting kisses. Slender fingers fluttered lower, pushing the waistband of his sweatpants down and out of the way so she could fondle the heavy sac between his thighs.

She squeezed it gently before curling her fingers around his thick, straining erection and then she measured his length with a slow, delicious stroke that made his hips buck upward and his hands clench the cool sheets at his sides.

Soft lips enveloped his shaft, surrounding him in a seductive warmth and a sleek wetness that felt so incredibly *real*. Her wicked tongue swirled gently, maddeningly, over the sensitive head of his cock, and then she took him deep inside her mouth and sucked. The strong, pulling sensation and slick, hot friction made him impossibly harder. His breathing grew fast, shallow, as sheer primal lust rose swiftly to the surface. The muscles in his abdomen flexed, rippled, and his groin tightened in prelude to the release he needed so damn badly.

A shudder ripped through his body, and he instinctively reached down to wrap his aching shaft in his own fist to take himself to completion. Instead, he encountered soft, silky strands of hair. Struggling between waking up and the drugging fantasy seducing him, he cupped the back of her head in his palm and rode with the pleasurable rhythm of her mouth and hands drawing him closer and closer to the edge.

Natalie…

The name ricocheted through his head, penetrating the fog of desire clouding his brain with the jolting realization that this was no figment of his imagination, but reality in its purest, most erotic form. His eyes opened with a start, and he found Natalie pleasuring him, confirming what his subconscious had been trying to tell him.

With an explicit curse, he tangled his fingers in her hair, pulled her mouth away, and hauled her back up the length of the bed so that they were face-to-face. He stared down at her, seeing her features through the pale light of dawn seeping into the room. Her eyes were wide and startled by his abrupt move, but she looked completely lucid. And so damn sexy and beautiful he wanted to take her right then and there. Hard and fast and mindlessly.

But his personal ethics wouldn't allow it to happen, despite that she was still completely naked from last night and didn't seem inclined to refuse him anything.

"What are you doing?" he asked, his voice raw and hoarse. Stupid question considering he was still throbbing from her talented ministrations, but it was the only thing he could bring himself to ask at the moment.

A sensual smile curved her lips, which were still wet from pleasuring him. "I was just returning the favor from last night." She reached down, took him in her palm and fondled him again.

He sucked in a swift breath as his penis surged with the threat of exploding. Grabbing her wrist, he pinned her arm at the side of her head, knowing he was one caress away from shooting off in her hand, which wasn't at all what he'd envisioned for his first time with her.

"Did I ask you to?" he asked gruffly.

The eager light in her eyes faded a few degrees as

she searched his expression. "No," she said softly, a quiver of hurt in her voice. "I wanted to. I still do, if you'll let me."

The woman had a way of crumbling all his defenses and touching him in ways he'd never, ever experienced. She was so selfless, so giving, and he was an ass for being so abrupt and turning her down, yet he couldn't take advantage of her generous offer under the current circumstances.

"After everything you've been through the past couple of days, I think we need to take things slow and easy for a while. It's for your own good." And his, as well.

Before she could issue an argument to refute his flimsy excuse, he scrambled out of bed, headed to the bathroom and locked the door behind him for good measure. He shoved off his sweatpants, his body still shaking from arousal and adrenaline, and his erection still standing at attention. He shook his head in disgust, knowing without a doubt he'd never make it through the rest of the day being so on edge, especially when he planned to be in such close proximity with Natalie.

Something had to give, and the logical solution was to relieve the sexual tension building within him. Taking a cold shower wouldn't even come close to doing the trick this time, so he turned the water to hot and stepped inside the glass-enclosed cubicle. He quickly washed his entire body and hair, then with the spray beating against his shoulders and back, he braced a hand on the opposite wall and encircled his rigid sex with his fingers. He pumped his erection through his tight fist, from the base of his shaft all the way back up, until his thumb brushed over the plumb tip and he trembled from the keen sensation.

He closed his eyes, recalling Natalie's soft hand on him, her wet mouth. He clenched his jaw tight, and three strokes later he came in a hot, scalding rush that ripped a low, guttural growl from his chest. The explosive feelings went on and on, draining him until he slumped a shoulder against the tiled wall and gulped air into his lungs.

The deed was done, his lust for Natalie slaked for now. Unfortunately, his need for her remained.

NATALIE OPENED CUPBOARD after cupboard in the kitchen, searching for a frying pan to make bacon and eggs for breakfast while fighting back tears of overwhelming frustration. She couldn't even recall where the pots and pans were, for crying out loud. Nothing seemed familiar, and she hated that she felt so weak and helpless.

She wanted to *remember*. She wanted to feel a sense of normalcy. She wanted to understand the conflicting feelings swirling within her. And mostly, she wanted to understand how Noah could be so generous with her pleasure, yet retreat and keep her at arm's length when it came to his.

It's for your own good.

His words echoed through her head, and another rush of hurt swamped her, adding to her tumultuous emotions. After this morning's incident with Noah, she'd been struggling to understand his actions and make sense of the upheaval in her own mind. Deep in her heart, she knew he was giving her time to accept her new state of mind and adjust to her current situation before adding the intimacy of making love back into their relationship. But dammit, she didn't need him to coddle her when she desired him, heart, body and soul.

While her mind, memories and thoughts seemed so fragmented, Noah was her anchor. He made her feel protected and secure in his presence, as if she honestly had a place where she belonged. And the part of her that felt so lost and disjointed needed to be close to him, emotionally *and* physically.

He was doing his damnedest to be honorable and noble when that was the last thing she wanted from him. He might have given her multiple orgasms last night, but her desire for him was far from satisfied.

With a sigh of defeat, she gave up on the frying pan and started looking in the pantry for a can of coffee, figuring that had to be fairly easy to find. Her search was fruitless, which only served to mount her growing agitation. Her chest grew tight with distress and her temples throbbed with the beginnings of a headache.

Minutes later Noah strolled into the kitchen, fresh from his shower and looking gorgeous and sexy in faded jeans and a beige T-shirt that outlined his broad shoulders. He took one look at her standing in the middle of the room with her fingers pressed against her forehead and immediately closed the distance between them.

With his thumb tucked beneath her chin, he raised her face up to his. "Hey, is everything okay?" he asked in that caring way of his.

She knew he was concerned about her, knew she ought to be grateful that he was so considerate. But at the moment his benevolence was the last thing she wanted from him and he became a perfect target for her pent-up irritation and confusion.

"No, I'm not okay," she blurted, throwing her hands into the air in a dramatic display. "I can't even find a frying pan or can of coffee in this stupid kitchen!"

Reaching for her, he gently pulled her into his embrace, and she automatically stiffened, not wanting to give an inch when he was the source of her cranky disposition. She'd changed into a casual, comfortable cotton dress she'd found in the closet while he'd showered, and the heat and strength of him penetrated the material, sparking a new awareness of him.

"Just relax and don't try so hard." He rubbed his big hands up and down her back in a soothing gesture and kissed the top of her head. His actions were warm and affectionate, but there was no denying he was much more reserved with her after their episode this morning. "It'll come to you in time."

"I don't think I'm a patient woman," she muttered, trying not to groan or give in to his persuasive tactics as he kneaded the taut muscles along her shoulders.

He chuckled softly, his breath warm against her ear. "No, you're not."

She ought to be offended, but he was so sweet she couldn't stay mad at him for long. He melted her irritable mood with his voice, his wonderful hands, his mere presence, and she finally let her tension unravel.

"You're bound to be emotional and sensitive for awhile." He let her go, then guided her to the oak table in the corner of the kitchen. "Why don't you sit down and I'll make you breakfast."

Because her own little tantrum had exhausted her, she did as he asked and settled into one of the chairs. She watched him putter around, finding utensils and food items with ease and whipping up a meal for the two of them as if it were a task he did every morning of the week.

Unlike her, he was back in control, his emotions and the awareness between them seemingly compartmentalized.

Fifteen minutes later he placed a cup of steaming coffee in front of her, along with a plate of scrambled eggs and crisp bacon. The aroma was heavenly, and she ate with gusto.

A sudden thought entered her mind and slipped out before she could stop it. "It's Monday, and I have a test at school today." She was so excited to recall something so mundane yet so crucial to her day-to-day routine that she grinned at Noah, who was sitting across the table from her.

He blinked at her in surprise, a smile of his own making an appearance. "Yes, it is, and yes, you did."

"Did?" She didn't miss the past-tense usage of the word.

"I don't think you should go to school today. It's too much, too soon." He took a bite of his eggs, then added, "In fact, you might want to consider calling the school and taking the whole week off. I'm sure your teachers will be able to give you your daily assignments and you'll be able to make up today's test next week."

She didn't think that would be a problem, either, but she was certain she'd go nuts without doing anything productive for a week, and she wanted, *needed,* some normalcy back in her life. "I'll call the school and take today and tomorrow off, and think about the rest of the week," she said, giving in that much. She took a sip of her coffee and nibbled on a piece of smoked bacon. "Aren't you going to go to work today?"

"Yes, I'll be working, but not at the office," he said with a shake of his dark head. "I've already talked to Cole, and I'll be working out of the house this week."

Finished with her eggs, she set her fork on her plate and sighed. "Because you feel the need to look after me?"

"I've worked from the office here at the house many times, Natalie, for various reasons, so it's not a big deal." Lifting his coffee mug to his lips for a drink, he met her gaze over the rim, his sensual blue eyes completely unreadable. "That's one of the perks of working for Cole. As long as the job gets done and cases are solved, he doesn't care where his employees work from."

Hearing the respect in Noah's voice, she smiled. "You're lucky to have such a great boss, and brother."

"Yeah, he's a good guy," he agreed indulgently. "I wouldn't be working for him otherwise."

"Have you been working for him long?" she asked curiously.

He looked her way again, the forkful of eggs heading toward his mouth hesitating a fraction, just brief enough to make her wonder why she'd caught him off guard. Until she realized that before her amnesia she probably knew the answer to her own question.

"I don't remember much about your work, other than you being a private investigator," she explained. "Maybe it'll help me remember something if you fill me in on the details from the beginning?"

"Sure." He nodded in understanding and swiped a napkin across his mouth. "After I graduated high school, I joined the marines and spent four years in the service. After that I goofed around with oddball jobs for about a year just to make ends meet because I couldn't make up my mind what I wanted to do." He grinned sheepishly.

She laughed. The bit of humor felt good and lightened the moment between them. "A rebel with a cause, huh?"

"I guess you could say that. I know I was a handful

for Cole *before* I joined the service, but all that discipline straightened me out real fast.'' Standing, he
picked up his empty plate, then hers, and carried them
to the sink. ''When Cole asked me if I wanted to go
to work at the agency to help him out, I thought, what
the hell. Why not? So, I guess I've been with Cole
for about, oh—'' he glanced up at the ceiling as he
mentally counted in his mind ''—seven years now.''

''And you enjoy the work?'' she asked, then
drained the last of her coffee.

''Yep, I'm hooked.'' After grabbing the carafe on
the counter, he strolled to the table and refilled first
her mug, then his own with the steaming brew.
''Every day is a new adventure. All the cases come
with a different set of circumstances, and nothing is
ever predictable. And the best part is, my hours are
flexible, and so is where I do my work and research—
like here at home.'' He winked at her, then replaced
the coffeepot back on the burner.

''Noah, the last thing I want to do is put a crimp
in your daily schedule,'' she said adamantly. ''I don't
need you to baby-sit me or feel as though you have
to be at my beck and call because of my memory
loss. I'll be fine. Really.''

''Sweetheart, humor me.'' Coffee mug in hand, he
leaned a hip against the tiled counter, his lean body
drawing her gaze and making her crave him all over
again. ''You scared the hell out of me when you got
hit by that car, and you can't blame me for being a
little bit worried about you.''

She didn't want to seem ungrateful when his concern was so genuine, so she didn't argue. Instead, she brought up another subject. "When do I go back to work at Murphy's?"

He rolled his eyes at her persistence. "You don't give up, do you?"

"I'm already feeling restless, Noah." She knew her anxiety had to do with not remembering certain things, but at least work and school would help to give her a better idea of what she *could* recall. "I need something to keep me busy. Something that's familiar and routine."

He eyed her for a long moment, as if silently debating her request. "Do you even remember what you did at Murphy's?"

"I was a waitress." That much was clear in her mind.

"Can't you just take it easy for a while?" He set his coffee mug in the sink, then crossed his arms over his wide chest, which accentuated his muscular biceps.

Standing, she dumped the rest of her coffee down the drain and stood next to Noah to argue her case further. "I really appreciate your being so concerned and protective of me, but I'd like to get back into the swing of things as soon as possible. I need to surround myself with ordinary, everyday things that are tangible to me, especially since so much is still so unfamiliar, like this house, living with you, our engagement…"

Noah averted his gaze, and Natalie wondered if she'd imagined the flash of guilt she'd seen in his eyes. She must have imagined it, because he had nothing to feel guilty about.

"I don't want to wait weeks or months to return to a normal life, or what *was* my life before the accident," she continued stubbornly. "And even though my memory loss unnerves me at times, I refuse to hide out here in your house, waiting for my mind to cooperate and finally rebound."

Returning his attention back to her, he gently caressed his knuckles down her cheek and along her jaw, his touch making her shiver. "You're impatient *and* obstinate," he murmured, though unmistakable affection laced his deep, sexy voice.

She smiled, but wasn't ready to give up her fight. "Tell me you understand, Noah," she urged softly, imploringly. "Your unconditional support is one of the things I need from you right now."

Shoving his fingers into the front pockets of his jeans, he exhaled a deep breath. "You've got my support, but I'm cautious by nature and it's a hard habit to break. How about we take things one day at a time and evaluate from there?"

His request was completely reasonable. "Fair enough."

He arched a dark brow her way. "As for today, can we agree that you just rest and relax instead of go rushing to school for an exam you might not be ready to take yet?"

She nodded, accepting the compromise. "Yes, we can agree on that." Pressing a hand to his chest, she rose up on her bare toes and placed a soft, warm kiss on his lips…and lingered, hoping he'd take the embrace to a deeper, more sensual level.

He was the first to pull back, and while his expression was reserved, she didn't miss the flare of desire brightening his eyes, or the growing erection pressing against her hip.

"I've got some case calls to make and I need to get to work," he said abruptly, and stepped away from her. "If you need me for anything, I'll be in my office."

She watched him go, then turned to wash the dishes in the sink. She'd hurdled one obstacle this morning with Noah, but there was another barrier she was determined to tackle.

Seducing her fiancé.

NOAH ENTERED THE NAME, address and phone number of Natalie's old landlord in Reno into his Palm-Pilot, along with other pertinent information he didn't want to lose track of, such as her previous place of employment. Right now, Natalie's welfare was his first priority, and Cole had assured him that the other cases he'd been handling would be taken care of between himself, Melodie and Jo. The reassurance allowed him to concentrate fully on Natalie's predicament and take the time to investigate the leads he had on her and her past.

He wasn't at all pleased with her insistence that she go back to work and school, but he understood her need to return to a normal life. It was unrealistic of him to expect her to remain cooped up in his house

until he nailed the source of the threat against her—
especially since she had no idea her life was in any
danger. And he wasn't about to enlighten her of that
fact and send her into a possible tailspin of fear and
panic.

He needed to find out who was stalking her, and
quick, because he had no intention of letting her roam
off on her own without insuring her safety somehow.
Going back to work in the evenings at Murphy's was
something he was willing to compromise on because
he could easily keep an eye on her while visiting with
friends and shooting pool. But until he nailed the
creep preying on her, she'd either be by his side, or
in the presence of someone he trusted. It could be no
other way.

Unfortunately, another problem still remained, one
that didn't seem so easily resolved from his perspective—and that was resisting Natalie and her tempting
sexual advances. That kiss in the kitchen, no matter
how chaste, had begged for him to respond, to indulge
in the passion they both knew was still simmering
beneath the surface, just waiting for that match to set
it aflame once again.

With an iron will that had astonished even himself,
he'd managed to escape the embrace unscathed, but
there was no doubt in his mind that there would be
many more sexual overtures he'd have to thwart along
the way.

The irony of the situation didn't escape him. He
wasn't used to resisting women, especially not one he
wanted as intensely, and for as long, as Natalie. He'd

always enjoyed everything about the opposite sex—their scent, their softness, erotic foreplay and hot, uncomplicated sex. For years now he'd indulged in brief, no-strings-attached affairs and reveled in his single status.

But everything about Natalie was turning complex and emotionally involved. And it didn't help matters that he'd lied to her. The fragile, tentative bonds of their relationship could be torn to pieces when she eventually learned the truth. She'd already questioned their engagement in subtle ways, including the fact that she didn't have a ring on her finger.

Resigned to crossing that bridge when they reached it, he pushed the troubling thoughts from his mind, picked up the phone and dialed the number he had for her previous landlord. He wasn't surprised when he hung up minutes later with no new details about Natalie's life in Reno. Most people were reluctant to give personal information over the phone, and this woman was no different. He actually appreciated the landlord's discretion, which protected Natalie's privacy, even if it was to his disadvantage.

Unfortunately, this meant he'd have to make a personal visit to Reno to investigate the various leads he had on Natalie and her past. He spent the next few hours clearing his calendar for Wednesday, then booking a flight and mapping out an agenda of whom he should talk to, and what he needed to accomplish in a day's time. He also placed a call to Murphy to see what the older man could do about putting Natalie on a light work schedule.

By the time he finished with his plans and other work, it was early afternoon, and it dawned on him that the house was awfully quiet. The silence was something he'd grown used to over the years, but he hadn't heard any noises from Natalie, which concerned him.

Exiting his office, he headed down the hall to the empty living room. He checked upstairs and the kitchen, but didn't find Natalie anywhere. His heart thumped hard in his chest, and he was just about to holler her name when he happened to glance out the slider leading to the backyard and saw her reclining on a padded lounge chair on the porch, basking in the golden rays of sunshine filtering through the overhead lattice covering. Her head was bent as she read the textbook opened on her lap, and she'd hiked up the hem of her dress to her thighs to allow the sun to warm her long, bare legs. She looked so peaceful and content, and his heart gave a tug of longing he couldn't ignore.

As he watched, she tucked her loose hair behind her ear and reached into the bowl sitting on a small table next to her chair and withdrew an Oreo cookie. She twisted the two sides apart and scraped the cream filling off with her teeth, then popped the chocolate wafers into her mouth, one at a time, and chewed. Then she licked her fingers for any lingering crumbs.

Smiling at her blissful enjoyment of the treat, he opened the screen door and stepped outside. Startled by his sudden appearance, she glanced up at him with an impish smile at being caught indulging in such a childish ritual.

"How long have you been standing there watching me?" she asked, a gentle accusation threading her tone.

"Not long. I was just on the way to the kitchen for a snack myself," he said as an excuse for spying on her. "Mind if I join you?"

"Not at all." She snapped the thick book shut but left it on her lap. "I'd love the company—and the break from studying."

He settled himself into a lawn chair next to her chaise. Confiscating a cookie for himself from her bowl, he ate it the *manly* way—in one big bite. "I've got some good news for you. I talked to Murphy and he said you can come back to work Thursday evening from six to nine, and you can gradually ease back into longer hours from there."

Warmth shone in her gaze. "Thank you. I appreciate that."

He filched another cookie and said very casually, "I also wanted to let you know that I have some work plans for Wednesday that will take me out of town for the day."

Her brows lifted in mild surprise. "Oh?"

"I hope you don't mind, but I spoke with Melodie, and she's going for her last fitting for her wedding dress on that day and said she'd love to have you along for company."

A grin quirked the corner of her mouth. "That sounds like fun, even though I do realize you're making sure I'm not home alone for the day while you're gone.''

''You're absolutely right,'' he said, unable to deny the obvious, then changed the subject before she asked what kind of work was taking him out of town. ''So, what are you reading?'' he asked curiously.

She stretched her legs and wiggled her toes. ''One of my college psycho-babble books.''

Not sure what she meant, he inclined his head questioningly.

''That's what Murphy calls them.'' She shook her head, sending her silky hair swaying across her shoulders, and laughed lightly. ''I'm amazed at some of the silliest things I remember!''

''Do you remember your classes and what you're studying?'' he prompted, treading carefully with his inquiry, wanting to learn as much as he could without her feeling as though he was interrogating her.

''Surprisingly, I do.'' She smoothed a hand over the glossy cover of her book, then glanced back at him with a smile. ''I'm majoring in social work and I know I want to be a counselor to help troubled kids, specifically foster children.''

''Which is a very admirable cause,'' he said, meaning it. And her kind, gentle and caring demeanor made her a perfect candidate for the job.

She shrugged off his compliment. ''I've been there before, so I can relate to kids who are part of the system and don't feel as though they have a place where they belong.''

''Is that how you felt growing up?'' he asked, genuinely interested in her past, in anything that would give him better insight to her.

Natalie leaned her head back against the cushioned lounge chair and stared out at the landscaped backyard as she considered Noah's question, which stirred up a wealth of emotions and obscure memories that gradually became clearer in her mind.

She returned her gaze to his and tried her best to explain what her childhood had been like. "It wasn't easy being shuffled from one home to another. It seemed just when I'd finally feel secure, something would happen and I'd get sent to another home with another set of strangers as my foster family and I'd have to start all over again. After a while, you try not to get attached to the people you're living with, which makes the process less painful."

Compassion deepened the blue hue of his eyes. "I can imagine what you went through—I felt that way when my parents divorced, then passed away," he said. "What was the longest amount of time you spent with a foster family?"

She thought back, waiting while obscure recollections crystalized. "Two years, during the time I was sixteen to eighteen years old, and then from there I was on my own."

As she spoke, she caught a quick glimpse of a blond-haired teenager, and remembered him as the son of the couple she'd been living with during those last two years. More fragmented scenes projected in her mind, throwing her off kilter with recollections of fending off his advances and hating that she had such large breasts and a figure that attracted too much attention from the opposite sex.

Strangely, that memory contradicted the desire she felt so intensely with Noah. The need that was physical as much as it was emotional.

Another male face flashed in the dim recesses of her mind, but this obscure recollection came with an ominous, intimidating feeling that made her shiver. Unable to pinpoint the source of the threat, or place who the man was, she frowned and closed her eyes, trying to bring the mental image into better focus. Instead of a clearer vision, her head spun and her temples pounded with the effort of forcing memories to the surface.

''Natalie?''

Warm fingers touched her arm, startling her out of her trance. Blinking her eyes open, she glanced at Noah, who was watching her intently. Unable to put into words what her mind couldn't even process, she decided to keep the haunting memories to herself for the time being.

''I'm sorry. I got distracted.'' She sighed, not wanting to talk about her past with Noah anymore, not until she had a chance to dissect her unsettling thoughts and make sense of them. ''I've had enough sunshine and fresh air for the day, and I think I could use a nap.''

He nodded his agreement, as she knew he would. ''Good idea.''

She headed upstairs while Noah returned to his office, but instead of sleeping she tossed and turned in his big bed, trying to resolve those old insecurities about her appearance with the uninhibited way she felt with Noah. Just the thought of him aroused her, and she closed her eyes and buried her face in his pillow. She inhaled slowly and deeply, surrounding herself with the musky, male scent of him, which intensified the growing hunger to know him again in the most intimate sense.

After an hour of fitful rest, she finally got back up again. Feeling mentally and physically restless and unable to shake the sensation, she headed into the bathroom and brushed her disheveled hair before heading back downstairs. Catching sight of the small white bandage on her cheek, she decided to clean her cut and apply a fresh dose of antibiotic cream.

She carefully peeled the old bandage off with a wince and swabbed the small gash with peroxide, then opened the medicine cabinet to look for the tube of Neosporin. A bevy of male toiletries lined the shelves, and she sighed. Other than a few feminine items, nothing looked familiar—not the can of Edge shaving gel, men's deodorant and after-shave, or the box of condoms sitting on the bottom shelf.

Condoms? She jerked her gaze back to the latter item and frowned. Hadn't Noah told her just last night that he didn't have any protection, so they couldn't make love? Certain the box had to be empty, she picked it up and looked inside, only to find it filled with at least a half-dozen foil packets.

Confusion trickled through her, which was quickly replaced by a surge of anger. Dammit, why did Noah feel as though he had to shelter and protect her, even from sex, when the last thing she wanted was to be coddled and treated like a helpless, delicate female who couldn't handle intimate physical contact?

Noah thought he knew what was best for her, but he didn't have a clue. Her body and soul craved him in an overwhelming, compelling way that wouldn't go away until she had him. Maybe not even then.

Jumping on the opportunity that had just presented itself, she withdrew a sealed packet. She would confront him with the evidence she'd found and demand an explanation for his refusal to make love to her.

And this time, armed with a condom, she wasn't taking no for an answer.

6

NOAH WAS SO ENGROSSED in work that he didn't hear or see Natalie enter his office until a small square packet dropped right on top of the paperwork he was reviewing. It took him a few seconds to recognize what had landed on his desk, but once the knowledge sank in, his stomach gave a sharp twist of dread.

Reluctantly, he glanced up and found Natalie standing on the other side of his desk, hands on her slender hips, her eyes blazing accusation, and her expression pinched with impatience.

He inwardly cringed. Oh, man, was he ever in trouble.

"What happened to the bandage on your cheek?" he asked in a quick attempt to deflect the attention off of him.

Her narrowed gaze told him she wasn't about to fall for his switch in topic. "I don't give a damn about my cheek at the moment. I'd rather you explain *that*." She pointed a finger at the prophylactic so there would be no doubt in his mind about what she was referring to.

Very calmly, he picked up the incriminating evidence and turned it over in his fingers, taking a long, drawn-out moment to examine it and buy himself some extra time. "Well, I have to say that it looks like a condom to me."

"Don't be a smart-ass, Noah," she said irritably, and pinned him with a direct look. "That's not what I meant and you know it. I can see for myself that it's a condom. What I want to know is why you lied about having any in the house."

He leaned back in his chair and affected a casual shrug. Ignoring the hurt and confusion in her eyes was a tad more difficult. "Because I don't think you're ready to make love."

Soft, dry laughter escaped her. "Don't you think that's a decision I can make for myself?"

Feeling uneasy at the direction this conversation was taking, he stood and stuffed the client information he'd been reviewing back into its proper file and set it aside. "You have amnesia, sweetheart, so I'm trying to make the decision *easier* for you, and I think you need time to recuperate from the accident first." God, his excuse sounded thin and insubstantial even to his own ears.

"And how long do you think I need until I can handle making love with you? A week? A month? A year?" She rounded the desk and boldly maneuvered herself between him and his desk so that they were aligned from chests to thighs, forcing him to acknowledge her and their sizzling attraction.

As if he could ignore it.

That quick, he grew hard and stiff with wanting her, his erection fitting perfectly at the crux of her thighs. Her fiery mood and determination turned him on, and he knew he had to do something fast or he'd succumb to her seductive scheme. Just as he attempted to take a safe step away from her for much-needed space, she grabbed his shirt and held him in place.

She rose up on her toes, putting her mouth inches below his. "I want you so badly, Noah, I ache with it." She lowered her lashes and nipped lightly at his jaw, then used her soft tongue to soothe the love bite. "Stop treating me like a fragile piece of glass. I swear I won't break."

Bracing his hands on either side of her hips on the desk to keep from touching her, he shuddered and groaned, holding fast to his dwindling resolve. "Natalie—"

"Don't tell me no." The plea was heartfelt and brimmed with a wealth of emotion as her lips traveled up to his ear. "I need the closeness and intimacy of making love with you. I might have lost parts of my memory, but not my desire for you. That's stronger than ever."

Noah squeezed his eyes shut as he battled between right and wrong. The words she'd just spoken were so honest, saying so much about her feelings for him—that while she'd turned him down for nine months, her indifference had been a ruse. She'd wanted him, too, and without those memories of keeping her distance, she was allowing her emotions and passions to run wild and free.

Seemingly taking his silence as acquiescence, she

pulled his shirt from the waistband of his jeans, shoved it up and over his head and tossed it to the floor at their feet. She flattened her palms on his bare chest, and her breathing deepened as she caressed his taut, heated flesh and strummed her fingers down to his hard abdomen.

Arousal surged through his bloodstream and arrowed straight to his groin. His erection pulsed against the fly of his snug jeans, making a mockery of the release he'd given himself that morning in the shower.

Bolder still, she dragged her tongue along the shell of his ear, then dipped inside. "I'm wet with the thought of having you deep inside of me, Noah," she said huskily, and lifted one of her legs high along his thigh so that she could rub herself against his erection. "Touch me and you'll see for yourself."

His fingers curled into tight fists against the hardwood desk as he fought the temptation to obey her request.

She gave him no choice. Grabbing his wrist, she slid his hand under the hem of her dress and up her smooth thigh, then pressed his fingers against the damp panel of cotton covering her mound. "Oh, yes," she breathed, a pleased, dreamy smile tipping the corner of her mouth.

He swallowed hard, which did nothing to calm the chaotic buzz of lust and need clamoring inside him. She was so damned brazen and sensual, her feminine confidence affecting him on a purely masculine level that made him want to drive into her, hard and fast and deep. She trusted him to take her body, to give her the physical intimacy she craved—he could see the certainty in her eyes, her expression beckoning him to fulfill every one of her sexual fantasies.

And he knew in that moment that he wouldn't be able to refuse her this time—wouldn't be able to refuse himself, no matter how wrong it might be to make love to her. Her memory might be skewed, but her desire for him was very real. And that's all he needed to know to assuage his own misgivings and set his hunger for her free.

Without warning, he lowered his head, crushed his lips to hers and swallowed her gasp of surprise. It took her only a handful of seconds to respond to his rapacious kiss, to welcome the thrust of his tongue into the silky, heated depths of her mouth. As they both indulged in the rough, delicious embrace, he knew there would be nothing slow, romantic or easy about this first joining.

Without breaking their kiss, he reached behind her and ruthlessly swept aside the items on his desk. Grasping her waist in his hands, he lifted her up onto the surface, heedless of the cramped space offered by the desk cluttered with his computer and other office paraphernalia. They wouldn't need much room for what he had in mind.

With his mouth, lips and tongue consuming hers, he shoved the skirt of her dress up to her hips and out of the way. He pushed her knees apart, spreading her legs so that he fit in between and his throbbing erection nestled at the heart of her femininity. She locked her feet against the back of his hardened thighs to hold him in place, and gyrated her hips in a slow, circular motion. He felt the heat and dewy moisture from her panties saturating through the denim of his jeans, and he growled at the raw, untamed sensation that ripped through him.

Abruptly, she ended the kiss and leaned back, bracing her hands on the desk behind her. Her chest rose and fell rapidly as she panted for breath, and her eyes were heavy lidded with arousal, the irises a sultry shade of blue. "Open the front of my dress, Noah," she whispered invitingly. "I want your mouth on my breasts."

He didn't hesitate, and immediately tackled the buttons that kept her so modestly covered. Once the blouse portion of her dress was undone, he spread the sides open wide. Leaning forward, he lavished kisses over the soft swells of her breasts overflowing her bra and dipped his tongue along the deep cleavage in between.

She shivered and reverently whispered his name.

Wanting her upper body naked, he pulled the dress and straps of her bra off her shoulders and down her arms until her breasts were bared and the bunched material tightened at the crease of her elbow. She shifted, trying to lift her hands from the desk so that she could slip out of the sleeves, but he stopped her before she could follow through on her intent.

"Don't move," he ordered, liking the way her current position kept him in total control. "I want you to keep your hands right where they are."

Excitement glowed in her gaze and her skin flushed in anticipation. Burying a hand into her thick hair, he tangled his fingers through the soft strands and tugged her head back so that her slender throat was completely exposed to him. Driven by something primitive and possessive that overruled his common sense, he placed his open mouth on her arched neck and grazed his tongue across her delicate skin. He found a particular sensitive spot that made her shiver and drew that tender flesh between his teeth. He nipped and suckled, and did something he'd never, ever done to any other woman—he marked Natalie as his.

She gasped and arched into him as he bit her neck, and he felt her tight nipples stab against his chest, demanding their own fair share of attention. His free hand molded to one full, straining breast, and his thumb and forefinger closed over the pearled tip and tugged, hard enough to make her suck in a swift, startled breath of air.

He continued to nuzzle her throat, then trailed hot, damp kisses lower. Finding her breasts, he curled his tongue around a waiting nipple, licked at her slowly, then drew her deep into his mouth with a soft, wet, pulling suction that made her thighs clench his flanks and her hips rock rhythmically against his thickening penis.

"Noah, *please*," she urged on a long, drawn-out moan.

With the urgent plea in her smoky voice and the sexy, provocative gyration of her hips, she brought him to the brink of climax. Without preamble, he reached beneath the skirt of her dress and yanked her panties down and off her legs. One touch of his fingers against the slick folds of her sex told him she was beyond ready for him and any other foreplay was unnecessary.

He reached for his belt, his movements frenzied as he jerked at the buckle and pulled the strap free. The steel button and zipper followed, and he shoved his pants over his hips, just low enough to free his shaft. Grabbing the foil packet that had started this sexual encounter, he quickly rolled the rubber on. When he glanced back up he found Natalie watching him, taking in his size and length with an appreciative lick of her lips.

Her arms and hands were still propped behind her on the desk as he'd ordered, and she looked completely wanton with her top open and her naked breasts quivering. Her dress was hiked up around her splayed thighs, giving him an unobstructed view of the pink, pouty lips down there, glistening with her dewy essence—all his for the taking.

Cupping her luscious bottom in his hands, he pulled her hips to the very edge of the desk, positioning her for his possession and forcing her to press her knees against his waist for better leverage. Taking his cock in his hand, he rubbed the taut, swollen head through her petal-soft folds of flesh, bathing the tip in slick moisture before ending the torment and pushing into her with one long, hard stroke.

She sucked in a swift breath, and a raw sound of pleasure rumbled from deep inside his chest as he watched her body envelop him, surrounding him in wet heat, and felt the exquisite squeeze of her inner muscles.

The sheer bliss of finally being inside of her was so intense, so startling, he had to take a moment to savor the feeling because he knew it was only a matter of a few strokes before he'd come. His skin burned, his muscles ached, and his stomach constricted with the need to *thrust*.

Holding back, he lifted his eyes to her face, finding her lips parted and her pupils dilated with heat and arousal. Wanting her on the edge, too, he pressed his thumb against the hard knot of nerves between her legs, just above where they were joined, teasing her with feather-light caresses that gradually deepened to long, rhythmic strokes. Her body trembled, and he could feel her fighting the orgasm building within her.

"Noah...*move*."

He shook his head, denying her for the moment, not until he extracted what he wanted from her. "I want to watch you when you come." And he wouldn't be far behind, he knew.

She groaned, closed her eyes and gave herself up to the sinful, erotic ministrations of his fingers. She clenched her legs around his hips, her breathing escaping in short pants. When he felt her body draw tight and contract around his hot, rigid flesh he finally did move, and took her where they both were desperate to go.

Yet he couldn't seem to get close enough, deep enough. He pumped his hips forward and back, again and again, his every thrust heavier, harder, than the one before. His heart thumped in his chest and his pulse surged, urging him on, taking him higher, but it was ultimately her soft, keening cry and the rippling of her second climax that milked him to completion, leaving him drained and light-headed from the incredible, shuddering release they'd shared.

Stunned by the intensity of their lovemaking, he gathered her close, and she buried her face against his neck and sighed contentedly.

"Oh, wow, is it always this hot between us?" she murmured, her teasing tone bringing levity to the moment.

"Mmm," he replied noncommittally, because he couldn't bring himself to tell her it was their *first* time. "If it gets any hotter I think we'll spontaneously combust."

Her soft, appreciative laughter wrapped around him. "That doesn't sound like such a bad way to go."

Oh, he most definitely agreed, knowing he'd found heaven in her arms. And now that he'd had a taste of how good it was between them, physically and emotionally, he knew letting her go when all this was over wasn't an option.

NATALIE LEANED HER HEAD against the back of her leather seat and glanced out the passenger window of Noah's car. Absently, she took in the scenery as her mind wandered over the past two days. Ever since that evening in Noah's office when she'd seduced him, things had definitely changed between them, in a very good way. She felt closer to him, more intimately connected. He'd made love to her with his body and soul, fulfilling not only her wildest fantasies, but touching her with tenderness and the kind of intimacy she longed for, as well. And she had to admit that even he seemed more relaxed around her, less tense, and more affectionate.

They'd spent yesterday together on what felt like a date, and she'd enjoyed every bit of her time with Noah. When she'd insisted that she needed to get out of the house for fresh air and stimulating activity or she'd go mad, he'd hadn't refused her request or tried to tell her she needed more rest. He took her to a movie, a romantic comedy that made them both laugh out loud, and they'd grabbed an early dinner at a restaurant before returning home.

She'd gone upstairs to change for bed while Noah headed into his office to put together files and paperwork and make last-minute calls in preparation for his trip today. All she remembered was crawling beneath the covers, determined to wait for Noah so they could make love again, only to fall asleep and wake up in the middle of the night snuggled in his arms. She'd felt so content and secure, that just being cocooned in his warmth and scent had been enough for her. By the time she'd woken from a sound, dreamless sleep in the morning, Noah was already showered, changed and had breakfast waiting for her.

Now, the following morning, Natalie still wore a satisfied smile on her face as Noah drove her to Cole's to spend the day with Melodie while he was out of town until later that afternoon. When she'd casually asked him where, exactly, he was going, he'd evaded the issue with, "It's a private, confidential matter." She'd respected the answer as part of his job as a private investigator.

"Here we are," Noah said, his deep, smooth voice penetrating her thoughts.

She glanced out the windshield at Cole's residence, taking in the two-story house, circular drive and immaculate landscaping, none of which she recognized.

She sighed. "I hate to ask this, but have I been here before?"

He shut down the engine and hesitated, seemingly distracted, then replied, "A few times."

"I'm sure it'll come as no surprise to you that the place doesn't look at all familiar," she said wryly, and when he opened his mouth to reply, she beat him to the punch. "I know, I know, give it time and it'll come to me."

A sexy grin eased across his mouth. "It's good to know you're retaining some things, after all." He winked at her.

She made a face at him for his teasing remark. "Ha-ha. Very funny, wise guy."

They exited the car, and Noah tucked her hand in his as they headed up the walkway to the house. Her arm bumped against something solid at the waistband of his jeans beneath his untucked shirt, and she knew immediately what she'd discovered.

"You're wearing your gun." Her voice was as startled as she felt. "Is this a dangerous case you're investigating?"

He stopped under the awning covering the front porch and cupped her jaw in his big hands, his eyes warm and reassuring as they latched onto hers. "Every case is potentially dangerous. I always wear my gun when I'm out on assignment, and sometimes when instinct tells me to. I even wore the holster yesterday when we went to the movie and dinner."

Surprise curled through her. "You did?"

He nodded. "Yep. You were snuggling up to my right side, so that's probably why you didn't feel it, but it was definitely there." After letting go of her face, he rang the doorbell.

Seconds later, Melodie met them at the door, and as soon as they entered she immediately gathered Natalie in an enthusiastic hug. The embrace was warm and friendly and made Natalie feel welcome and part of the family. The sense of belonging was a novel feeling—another one she didn't remember, but one she liked a whole lot.

Melodie stepped back to give her a critical once-over. "How are you feeling?"

"Pretty good." As they walked into the spacious living room, Natalie glanced at the man still beside her and smiled. "Noah's been taking good care of me. He's a little overbearing at times, but we're working on that."

Noah's soon-to-be sister-in-law laughed, her green eyes sparkling in pure delight. "He never used to be that way, but I guess it just takes the right woman to bring out the overprotective side in a Sommers' man.'' She leaned close to Natalie but didn't bother lowering her voice. ''Take it from me and my experience with Cole, these boys like to be in control and tend to be a bit dominant at times. Then again, it's nice to see Noah so tied up in knots over a woman.''

Noah sent a mock scowl Melodie's way. ''That's enough, Mel,'' he warned lightly, then turned to Natalie with a charming grin. ''Don't believe a word she says about me.''

Before Natalie could reply, Cole walked into the room, his striking blue gaze checking her out in a reserved kind of way. There was no denying both brothers were incredibly handsome, but Cole was definitely the more serious of the two.

He smiled in greeting. ''I was just getting ready to take off for the office. I'm glad I got the chance to see you before I left. You look great.''

''Thanks.'' Absently, she touched the scab on her cheek from her cut, which she'd left uncovered for the day. ''I still have a few bumps and bruises, and my memory is still fuzzy, but I can't complain because I know I could be in a lot worse shape.''

''I know you're feeling much better,'' Noah cut in, his tone authoritative, ''But take it easy and don't overdo today.''

Natalie rolled her eyes. ''Yes, sir.''

''She'll be fine, Noah.'' Melodie waved away his concern. ''Quit worrying. I'll take good care of her while you're gone.''

Satisfied with her assurance, Noah glanced at his

wristwatch. "I need to get going so I don't miss my flight. I'll be back around six tonight to pick you up." He leaned down and kissed Natalie softly on the lips, the fleeting contact over much too soon for her liking.

"Be safe," she said, the words slipping out automatically.

He stared at her for a long moment, his brow furrowed, then he said huskily, "You, too."

His response seemed to hold a deeper meaning she couldn't quite grasp, one that made an odd sense of foreboding settle over her. Ridiculous, she knew, and immediately pushed the disconcerting sensation aside.

"Come on, Cole. I'll walk you out," Noah said to his brother. "There are a few things I need to discuss with you regarding this case."

With one last goodbye, the men left.

"Are you ready to go?" Natalie asked Melodie.

The other woman nodded. "Just let me grab my purse from upstairs, and we can be on our way."

Half an hour later they were standing in a well-known bridal boutique in San Francisco, surrounded by row upon row of white, frothy gowns, pastel and jewel-toned bridesmaids dresses, and other wedding paraphernalia. The huge, one-stop store was divided into sections, covering everything from shoes, lingerie and accessories to casual and fancy evening wear.

A young saleswoman told Melodie that they'd pull her wedding dress and let her know when the seamstress was ready for her final fitting. While the two of them waited, they browsed through the various sections of the shop and wandered into the evening-wear department.

Melodie shuffled through a rack of outfits and pulled out a two-piece ensemble made up of black lace pants and a matching halter top. "What do you think of this?" she asked, holding it up to her curvaceous figure for Natalie to see. "I need a few new outfits for the honeymoon, and this might work for a night out on the town in the Bahamas."

Natalie grinned, seeing the glow on the other woman's face and knowing her soon-to-be husband put it there. "I like it, and I'm sure Cole will, too."

"I think you're right." She draped the outfit over her arm and continued looking through another rack. "Do you have something to wear to the wedding on Saturday?"

Natalie fingered the soft angora knit of an off-the-shoulder sweater dress that had captured her attention, liking the way the fabric felt against her skin. She considered Melodie's question, thinking of all her clothes hanging in Noah's closet. Most of her outfits and dresses were more suited to everyday wear, nothing that was appropriate for a fancy ceremony and reception. Nothing to turn a man's head the way she wanted to turn Noah's.

"I don't think I've bought anything for the wedding," she replied, and smiled impishly at Melodie. "This loss of memory really is the pits."

Understanding softened Melodie's gaze. "I'm sure it is, but look on the bright side. It's a great excuse to buy yourself something fun and new. Why don't you try on a few dresses and see if you find something you like?''

Natalie liked Melodie's way of thinking, which lightened her mood considerably. ''I think I will.'' She plucked the sleek, sexy dress from the rack, certain the wine color would compliment her blond hair and skin tone.

The next few hours passed quickly, with Natalie enjoying a female camaraderie with Melodie and learning that they had a lot of common interests. While trying on outfits together, they indulged in girl talk, and Melodie had amused her with the story of how she'd snagged Cole for her very own. And when Melodie finally tried on her wedding gown and asked Natalie's opinion, she'd replied honestly that she'd never seen a more beautiful bride.

A melancholy look entered Melodie's eyes as she explained how she'd grown up without a mother, and while her father was very dear to her, it was times like this that made being without a feminine influence in her life difficult. Natalie understood Melodie's feelings, because she still felt the loss of both of her parents, and suspected she always would.

By the time they left the boutique midafternoon, their arms were ladened with shopping bags filled with bridal accessories and new outfits for both of them. The dress Natalie had chosen had fit perfectly, and she'd splurged on matching shoes, tasteful earrings and even new lingerie to replace her practical cotton underwear. She'd paid for all her purchases with the credit card in her purse, because she wasn't sure how much money she had in her bank account to write a check.

"Wow, I'm famished," Melodie said after they dropped all their bags into the trunk of her car. "How about you?"

"I could use a bite to eat." Natalie's stomach chose that moment to growl, and her eyes widened in chagrin. "I guess all that power-shopping made me work up an appetite."

Melodie laughed. "Glad to hear it. There's a café on the corner. How does that sound?"

"Perfect."

They walked along the sidewalk to the restaurant and requested a table on the patio since it was such a warm, beautiful day. Melodie ordered a club sandwich and iced tea, and Natalie opted for a chef's salad and soda. The waitress headed back to the kitchen, and Natalie absently glanced beyond Melodie as the hostess seated a nice-looking blond-haired man a few tables away from them, who was by himself. He looked her way, met her gaze, and an arrogant smile curved the corner of his mouth.

A sense of familiarity tugged at her subconscious, startling her. Frowning, she tried to bring the vague thought filtering through her memory into better focus, but her mind refused to cooperate. Her chest grew tight, her skin prickled, and she felt ensnared by the other man's penetrating stare.

Shaken by the overwhelming sense of apprehension taking up residence within her, she broke eye contact and returned her attention back to her friend, keeping her gaze on Melodie's animated features.

While they waited for their lunch to be delivered, Natalie listened as Cole's fiancée filled her in on all the wedding preparations she'd planned in the past six months. Their conversation and the glimpses she caught of the gorgeous diamond solitaire ring on Melodie's left hand reminded Natalie that she knew nothing about her own engagement or wedding plans.

Unable to help herself, she glanced down at her own bare finger, then back up at Melodie. "Have Noah and I set a wedding date yet?"

The other woman's eyes rounded in surprise at her question, but she quickly recovered her startled composure. "Well, uh, no, not that I'm aware of." She shifted in her chair as if the subject made her uncomfortable.

Natalie didn't let Melodie's odd behavior stop her from learning more. "Have we been engaged long?"

Melodie took a long drink of her iced tea before answering. "Actually, it was all very sudden...." She fiddled with her napkin, opening the folded cloth and spreading it on her lap and making a big production of doing so. "And with your recent accident I'm sure making wedding plans isn't a priority for either one of you at the moment, at least not until you're feeling better."

Boy, now there was a statement that was all too familiar. "You sound just like Noah."

"Noah's a smart guy," Melodie replied with a cheeky grin.

The waitress arrived with their meals, giving Natalie a handful of seconds to analyze Melodie's answers. All her explanations had been logical, but like everything else in her life at the moment, something was off. And no matter how hard she tried, she couldn't pinpoint the source of her own discomfort and uncertainty.

Melodie bit into her sandwich and chewed. "My lunch is incredible. How about yours?"

Natalie recognized a change in topic when she heard one, and let it slide. "It's good."

Melodie obviously kept her mouth filled so she didn't have to answer more questions about Natalie's engagement, and the silence prompted her to sneak another peek at the man sitting by himself. He was still watching her steadily, as if he hadn't taken his eyes off her since he'd arrived.

Once again, a shiver rippled down her spine, and despite knowing she ought to ignore his disconcerting stare and cocky, knowing smile, her gaze kept straying back to his table. She told herself she was merely curious, but she couldn't deny that something inexplicable was drawing her attention back to him, again and again.

"Is something wrong?" Melodie asked. "You look distressed all of a sudden."

Natalie drew a deep breath, which did nothing to diminish the tension within her. "It's probably just me, but that guy over at the table behind you has been looking this way since he arrived." Even now, while eating his hamburger, his attention was still on her.

Melodie dragged a French fry though a pool of ketchup and popped it into her mouth. "Is he flirting with you?"

"No, not really." There was no real charm to his demeanor, but rather he possessed an intimidating quality that made her feel uneasy. "He's just watching me in a way that's unnerving."

Melodie cast a quick, surreptitious glance over her shoulder to check out the guy for herself, then looked back at Natalie, her expression suddenly wary and concerned. "He's being rude. Just ignore him."

"I've been trying to." Appetite gone, she pushed her half-eaten salad aside. "He's just so *obvious*."

Melodie finished off her lunch while doing her best to distract Natalie so she'd keep her gaze off the man, though there was no denying that the guy's presence seemed to bother Melodie, too. Natalie breathed a grateful sigh of relief when he finally paid his bill and left.

"I'm sorry," Natalie said, wondering if she'd turned neurotic since her accident. "I'm probably just tired and making more of the situation than there actually was."

"Maybe," Melodie agreed, but there was something in her tone that made Natalie wonder what her friend had seen when she'd looked at the other man.

They paid their own check and stood, gathering up their purses. "I need to go to the ladies' room," Natalie said, wishing she could shake the restlessness settling within her.

"I'll go with you," Melodie said quickly, her tone insistent.

Natalie slanted her friend a curious look. The woman was suddenly being overprotective, and while she, herself, was overwhelmed by all that had transpired, Melodie appeared just as affected—and determined not to leave her alone.

Together they made their way through the casual restaurant to the rest room located down a long hall in the back. Natalie glanced around at the patrons, in search of the guy who'd been watching her, and felt ridiculous, though immensely relieved, when she didn't see him anywhere.

They slipped into the ladies' room, and since there were only two stalls, one of which was currently taken, Natalie went first, then switched with Melodie. She washed her hands and glanced into the mirror at her reflection. At the same moment, the man's face flashed in her mind, and without warning she was overwhelmed with a feeling of claustrophobia.

She pulled in a deep, calming breath, but her lungs constricted in her chest. She had to get out of there and into a wide-open space. "Mel, I need fresh air," she said abruptly. "I'll meet you out in the waiting area."

Before Melodie could object, Natalie exited the rest room into the hall...and bumped into a solid male chest. The impact brought her up short, and the strap of her purse slipped down her arm and fell to the floor with a resounding *thump*. She didn't move, too paralyzed by the sight of the man who'd been admiring her out on the patio. Now he stood in front of her, so close she could see swirls of gold in his hazel eyes.

He didn't move, just continued to stare at her, as if waiting for some kind of reaction. Then his gaze traveled the length of her body in a long, slow once-over, visually undressing her, making her feel dirty and exposed.

Her stomach lurched sickeningly, and she finally forced herself to take a huge step back, though based on his calm demeanor, she didn't know why she felt so threatened. But she couldn't ignore the instinctive warning rattling her.

Her heart beat so hard in her chest she was surprised he didn't hear it. ''I'm, uh, sorry,'' she stammered, her voice escaping in a croak of sound.

He blinked lazily. ''You should watch where you're going and be more careful of your surroundings,'' he drawled.

A sense of familiarity flashed in her mind, startling her. Trying to grasp onto a semblance of sanity, she searched his features, trying to latch onto something tangible, and failed. ''Do I know you?''

Slowly, he bent down and picked up her purse, then slipped it back onto her shoulder, his touch lingering longer than was appropriate. ''Possibly, in a past life,'' he said, staring at her intently. His fingers caressed the side of her neck before falling away.

A shiver raced down her spine like a shock wave. His touch made her skin crawl and his words were cryptic, as if holding a deeper meaning she didn't understand. A well of frustration took up residence in her, along with a knot of panic.

The door to the women's rest room opened and Melodie stepped out, coming to a quick stop when she encountered the two of them in her way. "Natalie, is everything okay?"

Thankful for the interruption and the presence and security of another person, Natalie could only glance Melodie's way. Her throat felt as though it had closed up, and speech suddenly seemed impossible.

Melodie wore a fierce frown on her face, and concern burned bright in her eyes. "Is there a problem here?" Her question was directed at the man and demanded an answer.

"Not at all," he replied smoothly. "The lady and I just had a run-in. No harm done from what I can see."

No harm physically, Natalie agreed, but internally she was still shaking from the encounter and so thrown off balance she wondered if she'd recover.

With a pleasant nod to her, he moved around Melodie and strode down the hallway and back into the dining area of the restaurant. Natalie felt so light-headed and weak she feared her legs would give out on her.

Melodie placed a comforting hand on her arm. "Good Lord, Natalie, you're as pale as a ghost and you're trembling. Do you know him?"

Possibly, in a past life. She still couldn't make sense of his comment, so she didn't bother sharing his remark. "I don't know."

Melodie eyed her critically. "You know what? I think you've had enough excitement for the day. Let's get out of here. I'm taking you back to Cole's and you can rest there until Noah comes to pick you up."

Natalie followed Melodie out of the restaurant, too grateful for her insight to argue.

7

NOAH'S DAY IN RENO had been a long one, but very productive, and for that he couldn't complain, despite the disturbing details of Natalie's past he'd uncovered. After his flight had touched down in Oakland, he'd decided to swing by the office and update Cole on the information he'd discovered, and get his brother's input on Natalie's predicament.

Sitting in one of the chairs directly in front of Cole's desk, Noah told him what he'd learned from Natalie's ex-landlady, an older woman named Vivian who'd seemed genuinely fond of Natalie and concerned about her welfare. Once he'd shown proof of his identity as a private investigator and explained that Natalie's life was possibly in jeopardy, the woman had offered him a wealth of valuable information that had been incredibly helpful.

Now Noah passed on the details of their meeting to Cole. "While Natalie was attending college at the University of Nevada, Reno, she started dating a coed by the name of Chad Freeman," he said, recanting what the older woman had shared with him, while at the same time trying not to let the rage he'd experienced during the conversation with Vivian resurface again. "According to what the woman witnessed, the relationship started out well enough, but gradually she saw a change in Chad, who became more domineering and possessive of Natalie."

Cole rubbed a hand along his jaw as he considered that information for a moment. "Did the landlady see any signs of abuse?"

Noah shook his head, though his stomach constricted at just how badly she'd been mistreated. "No, not physically. Vivian felt as though the relationship was more mentally abusive. There were times when she heard Chad's raised voice coming from Natalie's apartment, criticizing her, putting her down."

Despite Noah's best efforts, a spark of anger ignited deep inside of him. "Apparently, things turned ugly when Natalie took on a job as a showgirl at a casino to make some extra money. Chad couldn't handle it. They had an explosive argument in the hallway of the complex. He called her a whore for using her body to make money, and she finally broke off the relationship."

"Good for her," Cole said, his tone laced with disgust.

Noah's lips flattened into a grim line. "Unfortunately, Chad didn't appreciate being dumped and he stalked and threatened her for a few months, and finally attacked her one night after work."

"Holy shit." Cole sat up straighter in his seat. "Why didn't she contact the police to slap Chad with a restraining order?"

"I'm betting she was afraid of infuriating Chad

even more, and she feared what he'd do in retribution for her involving the police.'' Noah also suspected it was a classic case of self-preservation that had prompted her to leave Reno. "I suppose it was easier for her to pack up and start over somewhere new than to stay and risk Chad attacking her again—which brings her here to Oakland.''

Opening the case file he'd made for Natalie, Noah shuffled through a few pages of notes and came to a photo of a blond-haired man with his arm slung over Natalie's shoulder, his hold on her too tight and his smile too arrogant. A protective instinct flared hot and bright in Noah's veins. He hated that the creep had ever tainted Natalie with his touch.

Shaking off the animosity seeping into his blood, he passed the picture across the desk for Cole to take a look at. "Vivian gave me this picture that was sent to her a few years ago as their Christmas card. Unfortunately I didn't get a good-enough look at the guy in the baseball cap who was following us last weekend to identify that man as the one in the picture. But at least this gives us an idea of who we might be looking for.''

Cole glanced from the photo to Noah. "You think it's Chad Freeman who's after her again?''

"It's the only thing that makes sense after everything I learned today.'' He rubbed a hand along the taut muscles in his neck and shoulder. "I also went to Freeman's previous place of employment and found out from the manager that he quit and moved about three weeks ago.''

Cole's dark brows rose in interest as he handed back the photo. "Do I dare ask to where?"

Noah tucked the picture into the file for safekeeping. "Not surprisingly he talked about moving to San Francisco, though the manager wasn't sure if that's where he ended up. But I'm fairly positive that's exactly where Freeman is."

Cole released a long, heavy breath. "So am I."

The certainty in his brother's tone caused Noah to frown. "Do you know something I don't?"

"Yeah, I do," he replied in his normal, straightforward manner. "Melodie called me after she and Natalie got home from shopping today. It seems there was a guy at the restaurant where they had lunch who was watching Natalie from another table, and he eventually cornered her alone where the rest rooms were."

The fiery heat of rage roiled through Noah's blood, and it took a good deal of effort for him to keep it under control. "Did he hurt her?"

"No. She was just shaken up by the run-in. As soon as Mel arrived on the scene, the guy backed off, but Mel was pretty sure it wasn't a chance meeting. She said he was just too cocky and sure of himself with Natalie."

Noah clenched and unclenched his fists, feeling helpless that he hadn't been there to keep Natalie safe and protected. "Then Mel got a good-enough look at the guy to tell me if he was Chad?"

"Probably so," Cole said confidently. "According

to her description, he had blond hair and hazel eyes, so I'm sure she'll be able to ID him with that photo.''

"Then I need to talk to her." The sooner the better. He scooped up his folder and stood, anxious to be on his way and to see for himself that Natalie was okay and unharmed.

"Mel will tell you everything she knows." Cole stood, too, and walked Noah to the reception area of the offices. "What are you going to do from here?"

He glanced back at his brother, so very grateful that he had Cole's support. "I'm going to keep Natalie in my sight at all times and keep a lookout for Chad Freeman, because the bastard's likely closer than we all think."

And for all he knew, the deranged stalker knew exactly where Natalie was right now, and that she was staying with him. The thought twisted his stomach up in knots of fury and frustration.

"Are you going to show Natalie the picture of her and Chad?" Cole asked.

He'd considered that idea on the flight back to Oakland, but realized it didn't serve any real purpose to present her with something that might work her into a panic. Obviously, seeing Chad in person hadn't jogged her memory, so it was unlikely the photo would, either.

"No. She needs to remember her past on her own, and I'm not prepared or equipped to answer the questions that would undoubtedly crop up if I show her a photo of the man who confronted her today."

Cole nodded in silent agreement. "Watch yourself, Noah, and Natalie, too."

"I plan to."

"DID YOU GET EVERYTHING done today that you needed to?"

"Pretty much." Noah glanced over at Natalie, who was sitting in the passenger seat of his car as he drove them both back to his place. "Though I heard *you* had a rough afternoon."

Her head rolled against the back of her seat to look at him, a wry smile pulling up the corners of her mouth. "You've been talking to Melodie, I see."

"Guilty as charged."

When he'd arrived at Cole's to pick up Natalie, she'd been resting in the upstairs guest bedroom, which had given him a few moments alone with Melodie to find out what, exactly, had happened during their lunch. She'd identified the man in the photo as the guy who'd confronted Natalie, which had put up Noah's guard even more where his pretend fiancée was concerned.

He now said to Natalie, "She was worried about you after that incident with the guy who was eyeing you."

Her shoulders lifted in a shrug as if the incident were inconsequential, but she didn't completely pull off the show of bravado. "It was all very strange, really…"

Her voice trailed off on a note of confusion, but

that didn't stop him from prompting her for more details. "Strange in what way?"

"The way he watched me while I was eating lunch, for one thing," she said, and visibly shuddered at the unpleasant memory. "His stare was just so... unnerving. And when I ran into him in the hallway leading to the rest rooms, the way he touched me gave me the creeps."

Every muscle in Noah's body grew tense, and his grip tightened around the steering wheel. "He *touched* you?"

"I dropped my purse and he picked it up and put the strap back on my shoulder," she explained. "His fingers kind of lingered against my neck."

He exhaled a slow stream of breath to keep calm. No doubt about it, Noah was going to kill the bastard when he finally found him.

"But what bothered me the most is that he acted as though he knew me, or like I should know him."

As casually as he could manage, he asked, "Did he look at all familiar to you?"

"I honestly don't know. I felt like I instinctively knew him somehow, but I definitely didn't feel comfortable around him. It was a weird contradiction I haven't been able to resolve in my mind." She sighed, the sound rife with uncertainties. "Then again, I think I've developed a case of paranoia along with this temporary amnesia."

He had proof that her apprehension was based in reality, so there was no way he was going to downplay the situation. Reaching across the console, he placed his hand over hers, giving it a comforting squeeze. "Do me a favor. If you ever see this guy again, let me know *immediately*."

She smiled at him. "You'll be the first to know."

Satisfied with that reassurance, Noah exited the freeway on the off-ramp and, after making certain they hadn't been followed, he headed toward home. They arrived minutes later, and he flicked on the house lights as they walked into the entryway.

"Boy, am I ever tense." Natalie raised her hands above her head and stretched her body like a lithe cat. "I think I'm going to go upstairs and take a bath before going to bed."

He clearly heard the invitation in her tone. "Go ahead. I need to check messages and give Bobby a call to discuss a case with him." Her lip puffed out in an adorable pout, and he knew the reason was because he wasn't following her upstairs. "I won't be long."

Closing the distance between them, she entwined her arms around his neck and aligned her curves to him in all the right, responsive places. "Promise?" she asked huskily, her gaze locked with his in a way he couldn't escape.

Not that he wanted to. She was a temptress, one he could no longer refuse. He knew what would happen once he climbed the stairs to his bedroom tonight, and he couldn't fight his feelings for her, or their mutual desire. The need to be an intrinsic part of her, emotionally and physically, was too strong to deny.

Especially after everything he'd learned today about her and her past.

"Yeah, I promise," he said, and lowered his head, capturing her mouth in a long, hot, deep kiss to back up his vow.

Once it was over, she gave him a triumphant smile and sashayed her way up the stairs. Halfway there, she glanced back down at him and caught him mesmerized by the slow, sexy sway of her hips.

She blew him a sweet kiss that found its way directly into his heart. "I'll be waiting for you."

It took monumental effort for him not to bound up the stairs and take her right then and there. Reminding himself that anticipation made for the best kind of sex, he headed to his office and settled behind his desk with Natalie's case file. He gave his notes a cursory glance once again because he wanted to memorize every single fact he'd unearthed of Natalie's past. The details would be useful in his investigation, and with Natalie, as well, when she finally regained her memory.

What threw him the most were the three very different, distinct personalities he'd discovered of Natalie over the past few days. He'd originally met a reserved woman at Murphy's, one who worked and studied hard, and didn't allow anyone to get too close. Now he understood why.

Today, he learned about the vulnerable woman caught up in a mentally abusive relationship that had undoubtedly cut down her self-esteem and made her more wary with men. A woman who'd chosen a solitary lifestyle over the warmth and passion that another intimate relationship could have provided. All because she feared her past would eventually catch up to her.

And now, at this very moment, waiting for him upstairs was a woman with incredible internal strength who was coping with the loss of her memory and making the best of an uncertain situation. Bypassing all the guarded caution she'd shown him before the accident, she now wore her emotions on her sleeve, openly trusting and believing in him. She didn't hold back her desire for him, either. She'd turned into a seductress, a blossoming woman giving into her sensuality and focusing it all on him.

Which was the real Natalie? The answer came easier than he expected. She was a fascinating combination of all three, yet there was still one facet of her personality left to reveal—the woman she would become when her memory returned and her life was no longer in danger. What kind of woman would she be when she finally realized that being with him was a lie, despite his honorable intentions to keep her safe from harm?

Closing her case file, he scrubbed a hand along his jaw, knowing that eventually the truth would surface. And when it finally did, he hoped she'd forgive him for not only fabricating their relationship, but for trampling across boundaries of appropriate behavior and falling headlong into deep personal waters.

Knowing there was nothing he could do about his growing feelings for Natalie but to accept them for the moment, he focused on business. It took him nearly an hour to return a few calls clients had left on his answering machine, and to talk to Bobby. He brought his friend up to date on Chad Freeman, and made a personal request to see if Bobby could find out any additional info on the man stalking Natalie. Specifically, a criminal record.

When he finally made his way upstairs and into his bedroom, he was stunned by the sexy vision that greeted him. He'd known from their conversation down in the foyer that she wanted to make love, and tonight he wasn't going to play hard to get or try to protect her virtue.

The damage had been done—she was his, and there was something to be said for the kind of intimate bond that developed between a man and woman during sex. He was ruthless enough to use carnal pleasures to touch her emotions, to steal her heart and make sure she realized how much he cared for her *before* the truth interfered with this idyllic relationship of theirs.

The woman lying on the bed, dressed in a silky nightgown that draped along her voluptuous curves and with a come-hither look in her eyes, had every intention of seducing him. Her hair spilled around her shoulders, beckoning him to sink his fingers into the textured softness, and a sexy, irresistible smile lifted the corners of her mouth. His groin tightened at the thought of making love to this gorgeous, sensual creature, to hear his name on her lips when she came—

and he knew he'd sell his soul to be deep inside her body again.

Unstrapping the gun holster he was still wearing, he set his revolver and leather holder on his dresser, his gaze never leaving her stretched-out form on the bed. "You look *incredible*," he said huskily.

She looked immensely pleased with his compliment. "I did some shopping of my own today, and I thought of you when I tried this on. I couldn't resist."

Neither could he. Her nipples jutted against the silky material, the tips as diamond hard as the erection straining the fly of his jeans. "I like it, but you do know you won't be wearing it for long, don't you? I want skin-on-skin contact."

"You'll get that," she said, and caressed a hand over her silk-clad hip to her bare thigh, seemingly enjoying the sensation she created—while driving him crazy with curiosity about what she wore beneath the skimpy negligee. "First, though, we play."

He lifted a brow, falling hard for this spirited, shameless side to Natalie. He'd play with her any way she wanted. "What did you have in mind?"

"Something…*erotic*," she whispered naughtily as her lashes fell half mast over her slumberous gaze. "See that chair next to you?"

He finally broke eye contact with her and found the armless chair he usually kept in the far corner to toss his clothes over. Now it sat prominently in the middle of the room. "Yes, I see it."

She smiled. "I want you to take off your shoes and shirt and sit down on it."

He did as she asked, toeing off his sneakers, removing his socks and peeling his shirt over his head. Leaving his jeans on as directed, he lowered himself to the chair and waited for her to choreograph the next move.

She scooted off the bed and slowly strolled toward him, the hem of her gown flirting around her slender thighs, teasing his senses. Lust rippled through him, heightening to an excruciating hunger when she came to a stop a few feet away from him, prolonging his need to touch her.

She wet her lips with her tongue. "Can you see the closet mirrors and the mirror over the dresser?" she asked.

He glanced from the closet to the dresser, realizing just how strategically she'd placed his chair. He had an unobstructed view of the two of them, at different angles. "I see the mirrors." He swallowed thickly, in near pain at the throbbing pressure taking up residence in his pants. "And I see you and me reflected in them, too."

She smiled in satisfaction. "Perfect."

He tipped his head, going along with her charade. "And why's that?"

"I want to watch you when I make love to you sitting on that chair, and you'll get to do the same."

Hedonistic images projected in his mind, of the two of them intimately entwined in the heat of passion. He groaned, knowing the fantasy would soon become reality, with both of them being voyeurs to each other's pleasure, and their own.

"All you have to do is tell me what you want, and it's yours." Her fingers glided over the full swell of her breasts, then she toyed with the thin strap holding up her sexy gown. "Would you like me to strip for you?"

"No, not yet." Refusing her request tested his restraint, but he knew how one look at her naked body could make him rush headlong into a quick tryst. Tonight, he wanted to take his time with her, wanted to savor and enjoy her playful, uninhibited behavior. "Though I would like to know if you're wearing any panties."

"The negligee didn't come with any." She shrugged, feigning an innocence that turned him on even more. "Was I supposed to wear a pair?"

Undeniable excitement pulsed through him. "Sweetheart, I'll take you just the way you are, which makes it nice and convenient for me." He crooked a finger at her, inviting her closer. "I want you to come here and sit on my lap."

She glided across the space separating them, and instead of sitting sideways on his thighs like he expected, she settled her bottom against his groin and leaned her back against his naked chest. Looking into the mirror in front of him, he could easily see how her legs were positioned primly between his, with her feet flat on the floor and her knees locked together in a shy, modest manner that contradicted her vixen appearance and actions.

The back of her head came to rest on his shoulder,

and she turned her face toward his, a sinful smile on her lips. "Is this okay?"

He settled his hands on her waist, just because he'd waited too long to touch her. And he wanted to make sure she stayed put. "It's not quite what I had in mind, but I'll make do." Wedging his feet in between hers, he drew her knees apart, spreading her legs wide open for him. The silky material of her gown draped along her thighs and covered all her feminine secrets, but not for long.

He buried his lips against the side of her neck, and moved them up to her ear. "Look in the mirror, Natalie," he said, and placed his hands on her thighs.

She obeyed, watching as he gradually slid the hem of her negligee upward until he'd exposed the soft, swollen lips of her sex. His entire body constricted with a sizzling stroke of heat, and he lightly ran his fingers through the dark blond curls covering her mound.

"Mmm, absolutely perfect," he said, his tone low and rough with arousal.

She squirmed restlessly on his lap, her breathing deepening. "Noah...*touch* me."

He knew what she wanted. Knew what she needed. But she'd been the one to suggest something erotic tonight, and he wasn't about to let her off so easily. "There's something incredibly exciting about watching a woman pleasuring herself," he murmured as he brushed his lips against her jaw and let his hands drift up her arms. "I want to watch you touch yourself. *Everywhere.*"

Hooking his thumbs beneath the straps holding up her gown, he slid them over her shoulders and down her arms. The shimmery fabric pooled around her slim waist, revealing her taut, heavy breasts to both of their gazes. Her large, darkly flushed nipples pulled tight with desire. With her wanton and naked on his lap and with longing darkening her eyes, she was the very essence of feminine sexuality.

And she was all his.

"God, you're so damned beautiful," he murmured, in awe of her grace, elegance and sensuality. Taking her hands, he flattened her palms on her breasts and helped knead the supple flesh with their entwined fingers until she picked up a rhythm she liked best. She moaned in protest when his hands drifted away to let her take over on her own.

"Do whatever feels good," he coaxed, and groaned when she rolled the tips of her breasts between her fingers and pinched them just hard enough to make her breath catch and her back arch into her hands.

And that's all it took for her to lose herself in the provocative fantasy he'd spun and to embrace her body's restless needs, to satisfy the carnal cravings he knew had her so on edge. Her palms skimmed lower, and he watched, completely captivated, as her fingers fluttered along the inside of her splayed thighs, and finally delved through her damp curls and into her wet heat with a long, slow stroke that made her gasp, shudder, and come apart.

Her head fell back, and a soft, wrenching cry escaped her throat as her orgasm hit, hard and intense. Her hips rocked into her fingers, and her bottom rubbed against his rock-hard erection, forcing him to grit his teeth to keep from coming with her.

Giving her a few moments to float down from her high, he brushed his lips along her flushed cheek and gently fondled her breasts to maximize her pleasure until the last of the shock waves rippling through her body receded. Finally, she went lax against him, her lashes fluttered back open, and she met his gaze in the mirror with a lazy, replete smile.

Turning her head to look up at him, she lifted a hand and trailed her fingers along his jaw. "My plan was to have my way with *you*."

Catching her wrist in a gentle hold, he brought her hand to his mouth so he could deliberately nibble and lick the taste of her off her fingers. "Here's your chance," he murmured with a wicked grin. "Finish undressing me."

Obeying his request, she slid to the floor in front of him. She removed her gown, tossed it aside, and pushing his knees open, she moved in between. Slowly, deliberately, she eased the tab of his zipper down and over the thick shaft stretching tight the front of his jeans, then she grasped the waistband and pulled both his pants and briefs down his legs and off, leaving him just as naked as she was.

Wetting her lips with her tongue as if he were a sensual feast she was about to devour, she encircled his hard length with her soft, slender fingers and squeezed his erect flesh. A drop of pre-come appeared, and she used her thumb to spread the silky bead of moisture over the broad tip of his penis and along the ridge of his shaft. His stomach muscles flexed, his cock pulsed in response, and a lustful groan rumbled in his chest, encouraging her to continue.

The sweetest, most seductive smile appeared on her lips. ''Now it's your turn to watch,'' she said, and took him into her mouth.

He sucked in a swift breath as the overwhelming sensations of slick heat and electrifying pleasure overwhelmed him. With effort, he dragged his gaze back to the mirror, taking in the woman kneeling in front of him and the erotic vision he was a part of. As she swayed forward to take him deeper, her hair swept across her cheek, blocking his view. Caught up in the fantasy she'd created, he gathered the soft strands into his fist and drew it away from her face, giving him an unobstructed view of her making love to him in such a generous way.

The last time she'd pleasured him, he'd believed it was all a lascivious dream. Now he enjoyed every bit of reality—of having her soft lips surrounding him, mouth suckling, and her wet tongue lapping and swirling from the base of his shaft, all the way up to the sensitized tip...until his climax sizzled just below the surface and the exquisite stimulation was too much for him to bear.

Groaning roughly, he tightened his fingers in her hair and pulled her away. She glanced up at him with dark eyes that questioned his reasons for stopping her when it was clear she would have gladly taken him all the way.

"I want to be inside of you when I come," he said, the answer coming from the depths of his soul, the longing to be buried in her tight heat and warmth both an emotional and physical need. "Straddle my waist and ride me, Natalie."

She reached over to the dresser and grabbed the small square packet she must have put there before he arrived. She quickly sheathed him with the condom, then stood, widening her stance and moving over his thighs so she could sit astride his lap. With her hands gripping his shoulders and him guiding his shaft into her body, she slowly lowered herself, taking him inch by excruciating inch, until she was completely seated on his thighs and he was buried to the hilt.

She sighed but didn't move, and he understood the need to savor the moment, the perfection of their joining, the utter closeness, and the way she clasped him so tightly. Opening his mouth against her throat, he lazily licked her skin and dragged his hands down her smooth back. Once he reached her bottom, he pulled her tighter, deeper against him.

She gasped and arched, and he moved his hands to her lush breasts, pushing them up high so he could take them into his mouth. He laved her nipples, grazed them with his teeth and parted his lips to take as much of her as he could. Her fingers speared through his hair to hold him close, and he suckled her, hard and strong. With a broken whimper she began to move on him, hips gyrating, body rocking rhythmically, and he let her set the pace.

He lifted his head and caught their reflection, their bodies naked and entwined in the throes of passion. "Look in the mirror, Natalie, and watch as we make love," he urged huskily.

She did, her eyes a smoky shade of blue as she met his gaze in the mirror, then took in their intimate position. Her lips were parted as she panted for breath, her face flushed from arousal, and he strummed his fingers from her shoulder to her waist, causing her to shiver in response.

He couldn't wait much longer, and wanted her to be with him when he came. "Send us both over the edge," he rasped, and bucked upward, prompting her to move as well.

She picked up his rhythm, matching him thrust for thrust, and the pleasure between them grew, driving them both higher. A desperate, keening sound escaped her as the heat and friction escalated. Seemingly needing *more,* she wrapped one arm around his neck, aligning their bodies from chest to groin, and used her other hand to frame his face as she lowered her head and captured his mouth in a deep, hot, tongue-tangling kiss that mimicked the fast, hard, frantic mating of their bodies.

The intensity was too great, the tumult of emotions he harbored for this woman too overwhelming, and Noah felt himself falling headlong into a searing orgasm that ripped through him like an electrical shock. And then she was moaning into his mouth, and he felt her convulsing around his shaft, milking him, shuddering with the force of her own release as she gave herself over to him in every way that mattered.

NATALIE WOKE UP IN THE middle of the night with a start, her body flinching as if someone had physically jolted her awake. Her heart pounded hard in her chest and she was trembling from the inside out. It took her a moment to realize that she was safe in bed with Noah, and that being chased through dark alleys to a dead-end street had all been a bad dream.

A very *realistic* dream, she couldn't help but acknowledge, one that had taken on nightmarish qualities that even now, despite being fully aware of her safe surroundings, made her shudder. The man in her dream who'd chased her had taken on the face of the guy who'd been watching her at the restaurant the day before, and that in itself bothered her. She'd been running desperately, trying to escape him. The fear she'd experienced in her dream had been distinct and stifling, and continued even now as she tried to make sense of it all.

Unbidden, a brief image flashed in her mind, of walking beside Noah and her being pursued by the same man in her dream. More disjointed glimpses appeared, of her fleeing Noah's embrace in a panic. Blindly running across the street. Hearing the slam of brakes and the sickening impact of being hit by a car.

Then she remembered nothing else, though those images felt real and familiar. She tried to conjure more recollections, something that would better explain what she'd envisioned, but all she got for her effort was more fragmented pieces to add to the already complex puzzle in her mind.

There was no doubt that she was recalling flashes of her accident, and she couldn't help but wonder if the man she'd seen at the restaurant had a link to her past somehow. And what if he wasn't only a part of her nightmare, but was connected to her reality, as well? She desperately wanted to remember details, but a part of her was also afraid of knowing the truth for fear that the sense of security she'd come to know with Noah might shatter, leaving her to flounder all on her own.

Doubts and uncertainties mingled with the other disturbing emotions her dream had evoked, and she huddled beneath the warm weight of the blankets, as if the covers could protect her from the oppressive thoughts and haunting visions tumbling through her head.

Noah shifted beside her, his hand absently sliding across the strip of cool sheet separating them. A frown furrowed his brow, and he blinked his eyes open. His expression relaxed when their gazes met in the shadowed darkness, an intimate, soothing connection that instantly eased the tension from her body.

"Natalie?" he murmured sleepily, and came up on his arm to get a better look at her, which caused the sheet to fall to his lean waist. He must have sensed her distress, because concern flashed across his expression. "Honey, are you okay?"

The man had the uncanny ability to know when

she needed him the most. His presence. His internal strength. And his intuitive ability to calm her when she felt so close to falling apart. "I had a bad dream," she told him, and heard the quiver in her own voice.

"Want to tell me about it?" he asked.

No, she really didn't, mainly because there was so much she didn't understand, and she suspected she'd look like an idiot trying to explain what she, herself, couldn't make sense of. So, she gave him a brief summary, just enough to satisfy his curiosity. "The only thing I can remember is being chased by a man, and I couldn't escape him." And she was so grateful that she'd woken up before he'd captured her, because she didn't want to think about what fate he might have had in store for her.

Awareness glimmered in his gaze, making her wonder if he knew the significance of her dream. Then he lifted the covers, beckoning her to his side of the bed. "C'mere and let me hold you," he whispered.

She couldn't refuse something so elemental, the need to be held and comforted. She scooted over to him, welcoming the shelter of his arms surrounding her. Snuggling close to his warm, naked body, she draped her thigh over his and rested her head on his chest. She inhaled deeply, and the male scent of him soothed her frazzled nerves and relaxed her, as did the absent way his hand stroked along her side and over the curve of her waist.

"Are you sure you're ready to go back to work

tomorrow night?'' he asked a few minutes later, his tone low and gruff.

His question didn't surprise her, because she knew how much he objected to her returning to work so quickly after the accident. She glanced up at him, taking in his gorgeous features, that sexy mouth that could curve into an irresistible grin as well as do incredible, wicked things to her body. ''Is there a valid reason why I shouldn't?''

He looked mildly annoyed with her argument. ''You know I think it's too soon, and after what happened at the restaurant this afternoon with that guy, I'm thinking you might need more time.''

And she'd use that time to sit at home and contemplate what she couldn't remember. Ugh. ''We've already talked about this, Noah. I have to go back, *for me*.'' She refused to be a victim to unexplainable fears, and she needed to move forward with her life, despite her memory loss. ''I feel good physically, and it's only for a few hours.''

He sighed, the release of breath ruffling her hair. ''You know I had to ask.''

''Yeah, I know.'' Stifling a grin, she placed a kiss on his jaw then laid her head back on his chest, amused by his attempt to be gruff when she knew he was as soft as a marshmallow inside. His caring and tender attitude toward her was what she adored about him, despite how overbearing he could be at times. No wonder she'd fallen in love with him and agreed to be his wife.

Love. The word resonated in her chest, filling it full

with the rich, precious emotion, along with the security of belonging to someone else.

It was the first time she'd thought of Noah in terms of love since being diagnosed with her amnesia, but the sentiment felt perfectly right, as did being a part of Noah's life.

She sighed, and cuddled closer, so very grateful that at least her relationship with him, and their future together, was something she could believe in and trust. Grateful, too, that this incredible man made her feel so safe and secure when everything else seemed so muddled and uncertain.

8

NATALIE SLIPPED A NEW DRINK order behind the bar to Murphy, then loaded her tray with a fuzzy navel and two bottles of beer to deliver to another table in the establishment. She scooped up a bowl of peanuts and gathered a few extra napkins just as Gina sidled up next to her at the bar to place a drink order of her own.

"You have new customers at table nine and fourteen," she said, slanting Natalie a quick, attentive glance. "Would you like me to take their orders for you?"

Natalie had only been on her shift for about thirty minutes, but within sixty seconds of working the floor she'd known that she was going to have to prove to her co-worker and boss that she was fully capable of handling her job—no coddling necessary. Unfortunately, she hadn't quite convinced them that she was more than ready to tackle a three-hour shift, and that her partial memory loss wouldn't affect her getting the job done.

Topping the fuzzy navel with a garnish, Natalie lifted a brow Gina's way. "Are you trying to horn in on my tables to make some extra tips tonight?"

Startled by Natalie's comeback, Gina's eyes widened. "Oh, no, of course not. I didn't meant it that way."

Natalie couldn't ever remember seeing the fun and frivolous Gina so flustered before. And if everyone didn't stop being so cautious around her, she was going to scream. "I'm teasing, Gina," she said with a smile, putting the other woman at ease. "I saw Noah talking to both you and Murphy as I was coming out of the back storage room before starting my shift, and I'm assuming that he was enlisting your help to make sure that I didn't overdo on my first night back."

"Among other things," Gina muttered, then winced. She instantly looked away and busied herself adding an olive to the martini Murphy had put on the pour pad. But not before Natalie had witnessed a glimmer of guilt in the depth of Gina's expressive eyes, which gave Natalie the distinct impression that her friend was hiding something from her. "What do you mean by that?"

Gina quickly composed herself and shrugged. "It's hard to blame Noah for being concerned about you. You are his fiancée, after all. It's sweet and you're a very lucky girl to have him."

Natalie heard the wistful quality to Gina's voice and smiled, though again she got the distinct impression there was more to her friend's comment than she was catching on to.

"Yeah, I am lucky," Natalie agreed, unable to deny her feelings for Noah, or how fortunate she was to have him in her life. "And believe it or not, I'm getting used to him being so protective."

Like tonight, he'd insisted on staying the three hours of her shift, just to be close by, he'd said, though she suspected his motivations ran deeper than the need to be near her. He was still worried about her state of mind, and that she might overexert herself and end up physically and mentally exhausted. Rather than argue, she'd let him win this minor battle, and now he was in the back of the place playing a game of pool with Bobby. The scene felt familiar, comforting even, as if he'd done it many times before.

"I'm fine, really," she assured Gina one last time, then picked up her tray of drinks. "I promise I can handle my share of the lounge or I wouldn't be here. And if it makes you feel any better, if I need help or feel swamped or overwhelmed, I'll let you know."

Gina nodded, and softened. "Fair enough."

"Thank you, though, for being concerned." Natalie felt equally lucky to have friends who cared about her. "It means a lot to me."

Before Gina could reply or the discussion turned too maudlin, Natalie left the end of the bar to deliver her drinks. After dropping those off, she headed to table fourteen to greet the three new occupants of the booth and take their order. The trio welcomed her back to Murphy's, and commented that they were glad to see that she was doing so well after the accident. While their faces seemed vaguely familiar, she couldn't place their names, but assumed they were regulars if they knew so much about her. She smiled and pretended they were old friends, conversing with them openly and easily about mundane things.

And so the evening went, with her working from table to table and keeping busy with the Thursday-evening crowd that frequented Murphy's. She felt energized and invigorated, and enjoyed the steady stream of orders that kept her moving and enabled her to shake off the restlessness of the past few days.

She delivered trays of drinks and appetizers, and was amazed and touched at just how many people were concerned about her. Some of the customers she recognized, others she had a hard time placing, but she managed to fumble her way through conversations without anyone being the wiser.

During a lull in business near quitting time for her, she made her way back to the gaming area to see if Noah and Bobby needed a refill on anything. Just as she arrived, Noah bent low over the pool table to make a difficult shot, and a keen sense of déjà vu washed over her. Or maybe a real, tangible memory, she realized giddily. Instinctively, she knew she'd seen him in this stance before, could recall admiring him and his firm, muscular backside in soft worn denim.

And it seemed very likely that she might have admired him in such an audacious way. Noah was a sexy, gorgeous man with enough masculine sex appeal to make any woman breathless with wanting him. Except he was all hers, and that knowledge made her tingle with warmth and anticipation of what would happen once he took her home tonight and they were all alone.

But first, she'd up the stakes of his game.

She leaned in next to his side, so close his arousing male scent surrounded her. "Make that shot, and I'll be your love slave tonight," she whispered seductively in his ear, just to rattle his composure and test his restraint.

He tipped his head sideways, meeting her gaze. "I'm going to hold you to that promise, sweetheart," he drawled.

"Oh, I do hope so." She winked at him. "But first, you have to make the shot." Challenge issued, she stepped back next to Bobby to give Noah the room to line up his cue.

Most men would have lost their concentration at such a provocative proposition, but Noah didn't so much as falter as he hit the cue ball, which connected with a red solid, pocketing the billiard ball with precision.

Slowly, he straightened, a lazy, disarming smile curving the corners of his mouth and devilry dancing in his hot blue gaze. "Looks like you're mine tonight, honey. Are you off the clock yet?"

She laughed as she picked up the empty glasses on a nearby table and wiped down the surface with a damp rag, noticing that Bobby was observing their flirtatious interaction with amusement.

"Feeling a bit impatient to be out of here all of a sudden?" she quipped, a naughty inflection to her voice.

"Damn right," Noah growled, low and sexy, his hungry eyes watching her as she worked.

She deliberately put an extra sway in her hips just for him. "Well, you're going to have to hold your horses just a bit longer, lover boy. I've got a few more minutes before my shift is over."

Noah groaned. "You're lucky I don't just haul you over my shoulder and carry you out of here, caveman-style."

"Now, that sounds tempting," she teased, wondering if he'd truly dare to be so bold, and found herself very excited by the notion of Noah being so sexually aggressive with her.

Putting aside those lustful thoughts, she returned to business, knowing she had a few more customers to attend to before she called it a night. "Any last orders for either of you boys?"

Noah shook his head. "Nothing for me. I had my limit of sodas for the night," he replied wryly.

"I'm good," Bobby said, eyeing the balls on the pool table for his shot. "After this game I'm outta here, too."

"Great." She turned back to Noah. Her stomach fluttered at the seductive game she'd instigated between them, and at how he might take advantage of his prize. "Give me ten more minutes to finish up with my tables, and I'll be ready to go."

With a spring in her step, and a few erotic scenarios of her own tumbling through her mind, she returned to the lounge. The steady stream of people had slowed considerably, and she filled a few last drink orders and cleared off the tables her customers had vacated. She tossed the empty beer bottles in the trash and set the dirty glasses at the end of the bar where Murphy washed them. Finished with her cleanup duties, she glanced around for Gina to let her know that she was on her own for the next hour or so.

The other woman was heading toward her, her own tray filled with empty drink glasses. "I'm getting ready to clock out for the night," Natalie said. "Can you handle things from here?"

"Yeah, I'll be fine." Gina withdrew a folded cocktail napkin from her apron pocket and handed it toward Natalie. "I have a note for you."

"A note?" Natalie repeated, suddenly feeling wary, though she couldn't explain why. She hesitated an extra heartbeat, then reached out and took the napkin, though she didn't immediately open it. "Who is it from?"

"A guy sitting in my section," Gina replied as she emptied her tray, then glanced back toward the corner of the bar. "He's right over there at that far booth facing the window...." Her voice trailed off, and she shook her head. "Well, he *was* sitting at that table. Maybe he went to use the rest room."

Unease prickled along the back of Natalie's neck, and though every instinct in her rallied against reading the note, morbid curiosity won over common sense. She opened the napkin, and her gaze scanned the words written in a bold, masculine scrawl: *Be more careful of your surroundings. I'm watching you and waiting to make you mine again.*

"Oh, God," she croaked, and immediately dropped the ominous note as if it were toxic. Her entire body shook uncontrollably, the tremors starting deep and working their way up to the surface.

The words *be more careful of your surroundings* echoed in her mind, and an image of the man at the restaurant saying them formed in her head. Had he followed her here to where she worked? And if so, why?

The questions came fast and furiously, but unfortunately there were no answers. Her head spun, an awful pressure grew in her chest, and an unexplainable fear clawed inside her, as if attempting to break loose. She swayed on her feet, desperately trying to tamp down those alarming emotions, afraid if she dared to set them free they'd strangle her.

"Natalie?" Apprehension laced Gina's voice, and she grabbed her arm to steady her. "You look like you're going to pass out!"

Natalie leaned against a bar stool before her legs collapsed and reached for the only lifeline she knew she could count on. The only person who might make sense of what she was experiencing.

"Get me Noah," she whispered.

"NOAH, NATALIE NEEDS YOU."

The panic in Gina's voice snagged Noah's attention, putting every one of his personal and professional instincts on full alert. Abandoning his casual conversation with Bobby, Noah searched the room for

Natalie, until he finally found her sitting at the far end of the bar, her face buried in her hands.

Without hesitation he started after her, with Bobby and Gina following. "What the hell happened?" he demanded, feeling as though a mile separated him from Natalie. He couldn't seem to get to her fast enough.

"I was waiting on a guy in my section," Gina said, taking two steps to his every one to keep up with his quick stride. "He seemed nice enough, and he gave me a note to give to Natalie. Whatever it said set her off."

Shit. "What did he look like?" Without asking, Noah knew who'd sent Natalie the note. But he had to ask Gina, just so both he and Bobby could document the information on an official report.

The quick description she gave him matched Chad Freeman exactly and made Noah's blood run cold at the thought of how close the other man had been to Natalie…and Noah hadn't even known.

"He was sitting at that far booth facing the window, and after I gave Natalie the note I looked back and he was gone," Gina explained, the contrition in her voice clear. "I didn't think anything of it, really. I mean, he knew Natalie's name, so I automatically thought she knew him."

As much as the situation made Noah's gut twist, he couldn't blame Gina for her actions. If anyone was at fault, it was himself. He was responsible for Natalie, he knew what kind of danger she was in, and it was his job to protect her.

While he'd informed Murphy and Gina of Natalie's amnesia and the engagement ruse, he hadn't seen the need to tell them she was being stalked. Not when Noah had been right there in the establishment to make sure she remained safe. Yet the creep had found a way to get to her, anyway. Dammit, he should have stayed up front to be closer to her.

"Maybe he went to the men's rest room," Gina suggested in an attempt to smooth things over.

Noah highly doubted that. Most likely, Freeman had hightailed it out of there after asking Gina to deliver the note. As Noah rounded the end of the bar, he exchanged a knowing look with Bobby.

His friend nodded in silent understanding, and said, "Go to Natalie. I'll check out front and the rest room."

Noah was grateful for his friend's assistance, but knew Freeman wasn't stupid. He wasn't going to stick around to get caught. He wanted Natalie, and he was teasing her, playing cat and mouse with her memory and her past.

The bastard.

Reaching Natalie's side, he gently grabbed her arms to pull her hands away from her face so he could comfort her, and she flinched at his touch. Then, seeing that it was him, she visibly relaxed, though the terrorized look that remained in her eyes nearly sent him over the edge with fury at what Freeman was doing to her.

Noah wanted to erase her distress, ached to make her forget the fear written plainly on her expression.

But first, he needed to collect the piece of evidence Freeman had sent to her so he knew what they were dealing with.

"Where's the note, Natalie?" he asked, his voice steadier than he felt.

"I…I dropped it," she said hoarsely.

The only thing littering the floor was a napkin, and he picked it up. He read the threatening words the other man had written for Natalie, which left no doubt in Noah's mind that it was just a matter of time before merely stalking Natalie wouldn't be enough for her ex-boyfriend. Noah jammed a hand through his hair, hating that Chad was so close to Natalie, knew where she worked and, quite possibly, knew where she was living. The man was so brazen in his pursuit, so depraved, Noah suspected he'd dare just about anything at all.

A shiver of foreboding slithered through him. He wrapped his fingers around Natalie's arm and guided her toward the back storeroom so they could talk in private, without worrying about prying eyes and listening ears. As soon as he shut the door behind them, Natalie turned around, looking too damned vulnerable for his peace of mind.

"I don't understand what's going on," she said, her gaze searching his for answers, her posture rigid. "Why is he doing this to me?"

He? Startled by her choice of word, he frowned. "You *know* who sent this note?" he asked cautiously.

She nodded jerkily and wrapped her arms around

her middle, as if trying to hold herself together. "It was the same guy that I ran into at the restaurant."

He narrowed his gaze, wondering how she'd made the connection. Had part of her memory returned? "How do you know it's the same guy?"

"That…that *note*," she spat, waving a hand at the offending napkin Noah still held. "The words that he wrote were some of the same ones he said to me at the restaurant. When I bumped into him, he said for me to be more careful of my surroundings." Her voice rose a frantic notch, her eyes wild with frustration and fear as she paced back and forth in the small, confined space. "And what does he mean that he's watching me and waiting to make me his again? Dammit, *who is he?*"

She still didn't realize that the man following her was Chad Freeman. Her ex-boyfriend. A man intent on terrorizing her and doing a damn good job of it. Her mind and memory still suppressed that traumatic time in her life. Noah clenched the note in his hand. And that left her too damn defenseless and susceptible to Chad's mental and emotional game.

Noah stuffed the note into the front pocket of his jeans, knowing that he needed to tell her what was going on with Chad, just enough so she could be more aware of her surroundings and protect herself. Her doctor had suggested that Natalie remember things on her own, but considering how easily Chad had reached her tonight, Noah would be a fool to believe that he could keep her safe at all times. If he armed her with the knowledge of what she was up against,

she'd at least stand a better chance of defending herself if the need arose. But he'd rather have that intense
conversation at home, rather than here at her work.

He reached out to her, gently wrapping his fingers
around her upper arms to stop her agitated pacing.
"Natalie, I need you to calm down."

"How can I calm down when nothing makes sense
in my life but you?" She shuddered and slipped her
arms around his waist, clinging tightly to him with
her face buried against his neck. "Everything else
feels like a disjointed dream where I'm lost and I
can't find my way back, and I hate feeling so helpless
and weak!"

Tonight, when he revealed her past, he hoped all
that would change, that she'd feel stronger and better
equipped to handle the threat against her. But one
concern weighed heavily on his mind. As she learned
about her past, would she come to realize that he'd
lied about their relationship? And would she hate him
for the deception?

For Natalie's sake, it was a chance he had to take.

BY THE TIME NOAH ESCORTED her into his house, shut
and locked the door behind them, then set the alarm,
Natalie was wound up tight. The awful tension from
the night's events spiraled within her, demanding
some kind of release. Knowing the one way she could
escape all the conflicting feelings wreaking havoc
with her psyche, she poured all her anxiety into sexual
aggression and focused it on the one man who could
make her forget, at least for a little while.

Not giving Noah a chance to refuse her or what she wanted, she threaded her fingers through his thick hair and pulled his mouth down to hers before he could anticipate what she intended. Their lips met, and she instigated a deep mating of tongues that was as demanding as her hunger for him. From there, it took only seconds for her fears and uncertainties to manifest themselves into a searing need that couldn't be denied. Aching to feel his heated flesh against her, she grabbed at his shirt and pulled it from the waistband of his jeans, nearly ripping the cotton material in her haste. But before she could shove it up and over his head, Noah grabbed her wrists, stopping her.

He groaned deep in his throat and pulled back just enough to break their kiss and so that she could see his eyes, dark and hot with suppressed lust. "Natalie...we need to talk."

Conversation was the last thing she wanted. Despite his authoritative tone, she could sense his control wavering. Could feel him hanging on to reason by a tenuous thread, and she took advantage of his weakness.

"I don't want to talk or think right now, Noah. What I need is you." She touched her fingers to his lips, so soft, warm and wet from their kiss. "I want to feel your hands touching me, your mouth on my breasts, my belly, my thighs. I need *you*, deep inside of me." Her request was explicit and shameless, but she didn't care. Being brutally honest with Noah was the only way she could make him understand the fierce need to be possessed by him. Not gently, but physically branded, so she knew she belonged to him and no one else.

"Make me your love slave," she whispered huskily, tempting and teasing him with a reminder about their bet at the bar.

His breathing deepened, his nostrils flared, and she watched in pure female fascination as his discipline snapped, unleashing a dark, dangerous kind of passion she welcomed.

The next thing she knew he had her pressed up against the wall in the foyer. With her trapped against his hard, unmistakably aroused body, his mouth came down on hers, swift and demanding. The kiss was rough, wild and unrestrained, and it excited her all the more to know that Noah wasn't going to hold back with her tonight.

Adrenaline spiked in her blood, rushing through her veins like a heated aphrodisiac, spurring her to a higher level of arousal. This time when she attempted to remove his shirt he let her, and with a little help from him, hers wasn't far behind. Her bra followed as his lips and teeth grazed her neck, and as soon as her breasts were freed, his mouth was there, drawing a nipple into his hot, wet mouth. He flicked the aching tip with his tongue, then suckling her strong and deep, instigating a slow burn in her belly, between her thighs.

She shifted restlessly, her entire body pulsing, demanding *more*. The air around them crackled with intensity, and she smoothed her hands over his taut arms, dug her fingers into the muscle and sinew along his shoulders. Releasing her nipple, he knelt before her. She sucked in a quick breath as his teeth scraped along her ribs and then his tongue found her navel and dipped inside, probing in an erotic, sexual way that made her squirm and groan and grow impossibly wetter.

Deftly, he unsnapped and unzipped her jeans. Curling his fingers around the waistband of her pants and underwear, he dragged both down to her knees, exposing her to his gaze. Without hesitating and instinctively knowing what she craved, he leaned forward and pressed his mouth to her mound and unfurled his tongue along her cleft with a long, heated stroke that made her gasp and tremble.

The pleasure of his intimate kiss was immediate and electric, and she tangled her fingers in his hair, unconsciously drawing him closer still. She tried to spread her legs wider, but couldn't because of the constricting jeans. Desperate, she tilted her hips, angling toward his sinful mouth for better contact. His breath was hot on her sensitive flesh, and his tongue slid deeper into her sex, finding her clitoris with unerring accuracy and stroking rhythmically.

She twisted mindlessly against him, seeking an end to his sensual torment. Then it happened, and her head rolled back, his name escaping her throat on a low, ragged moan as her orgasm ripped through her. A rush of liquid desire swamped her system and scorched her nerve endings, leaving her dazed.

Noah abruptly stood and braced his hands on either side of her head, and she caught a glimpse of his disheveled hair, the flushed color slashing across his cheekbones, the molten heat in his gaze. He looked savagely male, and as he leaned into her with the press of his hard, lean body, she could feel the length of him vibrating with sexual tension.

Without preamble, he captured her mouth once again, his tongue finding and tangling with hers. The mingled flavor of Noah's aggressive need and her own dewy essence was heady and darkly seductive, and she reached between the crush of their bodies and cupped her palm against the thick erection confined within his jeans. She rubbed the length of him, slow and firm, and felt him pulse and grow impossibly harder.

"I want you inside me," she panted as her fingers fumbled with the button and zipper on his jeans. "Right here, right now."

A low, primitive growl rumbled up from his chest, and he clamped his fingers around her wrist to stop her illicit caress. His damp mouth skimmed across her cheek to her ear. "Let's finish this in the bedroom."

His bedroom seemed a mile away, and her body was on fire for him. "I can't wait that long, and I don't think my legs are steady enough to climb those stairs."

He chuckled against her neck. "We need a condom," he rasped, obviously thinking more rationally than she was. "And the only way to get one is to head upstairs."

She groaned her disappointment, then gasped when he bent low and hefted her over his shoulder, caveman-style, with her jeans and panties still bunched around her knees. He bounded up the stairs with an agility that amazed her when she felt so limp and boneless. Once inside the room, he flipped her onto the middle of his bed, turned on the lamp on the nightstand and quickly pulled off her shoes, socks, jeans and underwear. In the next instant he shucked his own clothes, then retrieved a condom from the drawer beside the bed and sheathed himself.

She expected him to come up and over her and take her hard and fast, but instead a slow, sinful smile made an appearance and she knew that Noah intended to take his sweet time with her this time around.

"Turn over onto your stomach, *slave*," he murmured.

She rolled onto her belly, and when he told her to lift up her hips so he could shove a pillow beneath her, she submitted to his request, unbearably excited by the thought of engaging in such an erotic position with him.

She shivered as his fingers brushed across the sensitive crease at the back of her knees, then feathered up her legs. His warm lips joined in on the provocative journey, following the path of his splayed hands with damp, openmouthed kisses and gentle nips of his teeth. She arched her hips higher as his thumbs dipped into the crease between her thighs and grazed the soft, swollen folds of her sex. Then she moaned when he increased the pleasure with a slow, leisurely lap of his tongue.

Renewed desire took hold, making her tingle from

head to toes. Anticipation coiled low and tight, throbbing for release. Yet he merely continued stroking her flesh, his palms gliding over her buttocks, along her waist, then up the center of her spine. His hands were pure magic, his firm caresses as erotic as they were tender, making her grow restless with a longing to feel him deep inside of her.

She attempted to spread her legs to make room for him in between, but he straddled her thighs instead, keeping her legs together. He aligned his hips to hers so that his erection probed between her legs and slid along her slick flesh, teasing her until she clutched the bedspread in her fists and begged him to satisfy the aching need he'd incited. The head of his shaft found her core, and he slipped inside her an agonizing inch as he settled his weight over her from behind, keeping her pinned to the mattress with the length of his body.

He swept her hair to the side, exposing her nape, along with the vulnerable curve where neck met shoulder. Then he opened her hands so she released the bedspread and intertwined his fingers through hers so that she felt physically bound to him. His hot breath grazed her cheek and his mouth touched her jaw and glided down to a vein throbbing in her neck. His teeth nibbled, and she closed her eyes and shivered, her stomach constricting with excitement as she wondered if he intended to mark her again in such a possessive, carnal way. It seemed appropriate, considering how inherently primitive their position was.

She was on edge, frustrated that he was completely

in control while she was a bundle of restless energy just waiting to come apart. For him, with him. "Noah, please. Don't make me wait any longer."

"You feel so damn tight, so hot and wet," he murmured into her ear, then flexed his hips against her bottom, lifting her pelvis higher. The dampness of her own desire eased his way deeper, making them both groan at the exquisite friction he created. Then he withdrew almost all the way out and pushed slowly back inside her, until he was buried to the hilt and she felt impaled by the hard length of him. He pulsed within her, breathing raggedly against her neck as his mouth sought a tender place to brand her.

She quivered, waiting, and when he finally sank his teeth into the tendon of muscle at the curve of her shoulder, she moaned long and loud. Her eyes rolled back, and she felt the erotic pull all the way down to her sex, making her inner muscles contract around him.

Finally, he drove into her, hard and deep, wringing another cry from her. He thrust again, his hips working like a piston, too quickly for her to catch her breath. He groaned her name. A demand. A plea.

And she answered him with a whispered *"Yes."*

He gave one last violent thrust, spiraling them both into a vortex of all-consuming pleasure that seemed more vital than each rapid heartbeat, more essential than each labored breath she drew. She shattered right along with him, blinded by delirious sensation and intoxicated by his wild need for her.

For a brief time as they made love he made her forget the threat surrounding her. But in the back of her mind the fact remained that someone was after her.

9

IT WAS NINE-THIRTY the following morning before Noah heard the upstairs shower turn on, and assumed that Natalie had finally gotten out of bed. As for him, he'd been awake since before his alarm clock had gone off at six. He'd taken his own shower, had quietly gotten dressed for the day, then left Natalie burrowed deep in the covers while he headed downstairs. He wanted to get some work done in his office before she woke up and he finally explained her past relationship with Chad Freeman.

Last night, the woman in his bed had been completely and utterly insatiable to the point of exhausting them both, he recalled with a smile. They'd made love three times, and once their passions had cooled, peace and calm had settled over her. When she'd snuggled up to him and asked him to just hold her, he hadn't been able to shatter the cocoon of intimacy with a serious discussion. He knew there would be plenty of time for that later.

Like this morning, just as soon as she came downstairs.

With a resigned sigh, he put away the paperwork he was researching on the Internet, grabbed Natalie's case file and headed into the kitchen to make a fresh pot of coffee for her, and himself. He could use another dose of caffeine to get him through the next hour or so.

By the time the coffee was done percolating, Natalie walked into the kitchen wearing a pair of cotton drawstring pants and a blouse she hadn't bothered to button up all the way. Her hair was still damp and combed away from her freshly scrubbed face, and she greeted him with a soft "good morning," an affectionate kiss on the cheek and a sweet smile he knew he could get used to seeing every day for the rest of his life.

His heart thumped hard in his chest, the knowledge that he'd fallen in love with this woman undeniable. She fit so perfectly in his life, in a way he'd never imagined any woman could. For years he'd embraced his playboy, bachelor image, enjoying brief relationships that made no demands on his carefree lifestyle and emotions. No attachment beyond sexual pleasure meant no potential heartache to deal with, and that motto had worked just fine for him.

Until Natalie. He'd taken her in, made her a part of his life, and now he was in so deep every fiber of his being tensed at the thought of losing her, which was a distinct possibility. Their relationship, their affair, had been instigated under false pretenses, and it was only a matter of time before everything came to a head and she realized the truth. He could only hope and pray his feelings for her would be enough to repair any damage he'd done to her emotions.

She withdrew two mugs from the cupboard, finding everything in the kitchen, in his home, with ease after nearly a week in his care. "I can't believe you let me sleep in so late," she chastised lightly.

He poured the coffee into their cups, and she added the creamer. "You obviously needed it."

She grinned impishly, her eyes dancing with a mischievous light he knew he was eventually going to douse as the morning turned to more somber matters. "I guess I did need the rest," she admitted.

And not just because of their night of intense, sizzling lovemaking. The distressing situation she'd endured at work had obviously contributed to the stress and tension, heightening her need to work off the restless apprehension that had settled over her. She'd chosen to lose herself in sensual sensations, and once she'd slaked her lust, she'd been physically and emotionally wasted. After their intense encounter, deep, uninterrupted slumber had consumed her, which had been for the best, he knew.

She picked up her mug and took a sip of the steaming brew, and the opening in her blouse gave him a glimpse of the faint, crescent-shaped red mark on the swell of her breast.

He reached out and touched the blemish his teeth had left on her smooth skin, and winced in contrition. "I'm sorry about doing this to you."

"No, you're not," she refuted, her tone playful. "And neither am I, though I'm glad you're not leaving your love bites in plain sight for everyone to see."

Leaning close, he nuzzled her neck, inhaling the

fresh, clean scent of shampoo and mint toothpaste.
"I'd like to," he said throatily.

God, he'd never been so wild and untamed with a
woman as he'd been with Natalie last night. But it
had turned him on to claim her in such a brazen,
primitive way, and obviously it had aroused her, too.
Just thinking about her eager, shameless response to
the way he'd taken her the first time last night sent a
rush of heat to his groin.

Before he gave in to the desire to take her up
against the table for a morning quickie, he inhaled a
deep, steadying breath and switched mental gears.
"Want me to make you breakfast?"

"I'm not overly hungry." She set her coffee on the
table, then pulled a box of Raisin Bran from the pantry and a bowl from the cupboard. "I'll just have a
small bowl of cereal. By the way, I was thinking we
could go shopping today to buy a gift for Cole and
Melodie's wedding tomorrow."

He nodded. "Sounds like a plan." He leaned his
hip against the counter as she added milk to her
flakes. He let her enjoy a few mouthfuls of her breakfast before deciding to get business done and over
with. "Natalie, we have to talk."

She carried her bowl to the table and sat down, a
small, hesitant smile on her lips. "I figured as much,
since you said that last night before I distracted you,"
she said, and took another bite of her cereal.

He felt a perceptible change in her, a reserve that
was nearly tangible. "Not that I'm complaining about
your persuasive methods," he assured her, wanting to

be certain she knew and understood that he'd been a willing participant in their sexual encounter from the moment she'd kissed him in the foyer. "But there's something I have to tell you."

She met his gaze head-on, and he couldn't miss the uncertainties and fear that had found their way back into her expressive eyes. "You know who's after me, don't you?"

He felt as though he'd been suckerpunched in the belly. He didn't know how she knew, but he suspected it was mostly intuition on her part. She might have lost her memory, but she was a sharp, insightful woman, and it didn't take a master's degree to figure out that someone was following her, considering how bold Chad had been in his pursuit so far.

There was no way to soften his answer, so he gave it to her straight. "Yeah, I do. And it's someone you know. Someone from your past that you don't remember because of your amnesia. And you need to know who this person is so you can protect yourself."

She shook her head, her confusion and apprehension plain. "I don't understand."

As her lover and the man who'd taken it upon himself to be her guardian, it was his job to make her understand. No matter how painful the process, no matter that his revelations might trigger a flood of memories that would be the beginning of the end for them. He had to level with her, at least about her relationship with Chad so she knew what kind of danger she was up against.

He sat in the chair next to hers at the table, and

took a long drink of his coffee for fortitude. "Before you moved to Oakland, you lived in Reno. Do you remember that?"

Her brow furrowed into a frown, as if she were trying to recall that time in her life. "Parts of it," she said vaguely.

He waited a little longer for her to mull over the information he'd given her, but nothing seemed to click into place for her. Not yet, anyway.

He continued to feed her more facts, a little at a time so he didn't overwhelm her. "You went to college at University of Nevada, Reno, and you were dating a man by the name of Chad Freeman."

She set her spoon in her half-eaten cereal and pushed the bowl aside, her appetite obviously gone. "The name...it's familiar somehow."

But she wasn't placing the man's name with a face...yet. Noah knew he had no choice but to connect the link for her. Reaching for the file folder he'd brought into the kitchen with him, he withdrew the photo her old landlady had given him. He was all too aware of the personal risk he was taking by showing her the picture, bringing Chad Freeman between them.

But his choices were limited, and he wasn't about to sacrifice her safety for his own selfish desire to completely erase her past with a man who'd abused her. "This is Chad Freeman," he stated, and forced himself to turn the picture around for her to see.

Her eyes widened, and her face turned chalk white. "Oh, God," she croaked, visibly shaken. "He's the man who cornered me in the restaurant.'' She raised her gaze to Noah, panic and confusion etched across her expression. ''And what am I doing in that picture with him?''

Seeing how traumatized she was by the photo, he tucked it back into the folder. ''Like I said, you were dating him for a few years. He's the man I believe is after you, Natalie.''

She shook her head in denial, her shock rendering her momentarily speechless.

He hated putting her through such emotional turmoil, but her life and future were at stake. ''Natalie, honey, I need to know if you remember if this is the man you were running from before you were hit by the car.''

She squeezed her eyes shut and pressed her fingers to her temple, as if trying to conjure images in her mind. When she looked at him again, her distress was prominently stamped on her features. ''I...I don't remember!'' Her breathing had grown labored. ''Are you saying that an old boyfriend is *stalking* me?''

''All the evidence that I've been able to come up with leads to Chad.'' He placed a comforting hand over hers, not surprised to find her skin cool and clammy. ''He's getting bolder in his attempts, and you need to know who and what is threatening you.''

''But why would he want to hurt me?''

Because Chad Freeman was a deranged son of a bitch who didn't deal well with rejection, Noah thought bitterly. But he kept his own personal theory to himself, instead revealing to Natalie what he'd discovered from her landlady, Vivian. He explained how Chad had become more domineering of her and mentally abusive, and how his temper had exploded when she'd taken on a job as a showgirl to earn some extra money. When she'd broken off the relationship he'd stalked her and finally physically attacked her one night after work.

Disbelief and horror flashed in her gaze, and she abruptly stood up, her entire body stiff. "Why don't I remember any of this?" she demanded, her tone high and shrill and near hysterical.

Concerned that the overload of information he'd given her, all of which she couldn't recall, would cause her to have a nervous breakdown, he stood, too, ready to catch her if she fell apart. "According to the doctor who treated you the night of your accident, he explained that your retrograde amnesia could have been caused not only by a head injury, but by something traumatic you might have suffered before the accident, and that might have been Chad following you that night. As a result, your memory is blocking out your past with him and other recollections you might not want to remember."

"But I *do* want to remember," she insisted angrily through clenched teeth, "because I can't go on like this much longer!"

Unable to help himself, he gathered her into his arms, holding her close to soothe her anxiety and fears. "I've got Bobby working the case, along with me and Cole. We're going to find him, Natalie," he said fiercely. "And in the meantime, I'm going to do everything in my power to protect you."

Unfortunately, despite his best intentions and resources, he knew she wouldn't be completely safe until they caught Chad.

"BY THE POWER VESTED IN ME, I now pronounce you man and wife," the minister said, closing his Bible and looking up at Cole and Melodie with a smile. "You may now kiss your new bride."

Sighing wistfully, Natalie watched as Cole lifted Melodie's veil, gathered her into his strong embrace and gave her a kiss that had the congregation of family and friends applauding their new marital status. Flanking the happy bride and groom as best man and maid-of-honor were Cole's two siblings, Noah and Joelle, who were beaming with pride.

Joelle's husband, Dean, had opted out of the wedding party in order to take care of his daughter, and he sat next to Natalie in the second pew from the front with five-month-old Jennifer perched on his lap. During the ceremony he'd kept the baby quiet with a bottle, but now the little girl seemed to know it was time to celebrate the joyous occasion and wanted to add to the good cheer. She waved the rattle her daddy had put into her pudgy hand, shaking the noisemaker with enthusiasm and squealing delightedly for good measure.

Natalie laughed, completely charmed by the sweet baby and the obvious affection between father and daughter. Dean was a doting daddy, and she felt so fortunate to be a part of the close, loving dynamics of the Sommers family.

After the upsetting day she'd had yesterday since discovering that a sadistic ex-boyfriend was stalking her, and after experiencing vague recollections of her past with Chad throughout the afternoon and evening, Natalie was grateful for the reprieve of Cole and Melodie's wedding. Despite the occasional concerned glance Noah cast her way to make sure she was doing okay, the day was filled with joy, laughter and an abundance of smiles, and the cheerful atmosphere made her forget about her own problems for a little while.

With the ceremony over, the wedding party and guests poured out of the church and followed the bride and groom to a nearby country club for the reception. The ballroom was huge, filled with white streamers, iridescent balloons and lush, fragrant floral bouquets on every table. Cole and Melodie sat up on a higher platform, just the two of them, while the bridesmaids and groomsmen were able to sit at a reserved table up front with their significant others.

Finally, after all his best-man obligations were fulfilled, Noah settled into the chair beside hers, looking breathtakingly handsome in his formal black tuxedo and lavender bow tie that matched the bridesmaids' gowns. His striking blue eyes glimmered with enjoyment, and he wore a bad-boy grin just for her that jump-started her pulse.

He dipped his head close to hers, and his warm male scent added to the desire settling low and deep within her. "Have I told you how incredibly sexy you look in that dress?" He trailed a finger along the line of her shoulder, bared by the design of the outfit.

She shivered at his seductive touch and welcomed his playful charm, immensely pleased that he liked the sleek, wine-colored dress she'd chosen with him in mind. "You've told me, oh, only about a dozen times."

Beneath the table, he flattened his hand on her knee and skimmed his hot palm under the hem of her dress and up her thigh. "But what I haven't told you is that I can't wait to find out what you're wearing *beneath* it."

His boldness caught her off guard, considering they were seated with four other couples and his baby niece was nearby. She clamped her legs together before he could discover that the only things separating his searching fingers from her flesh were thigh-high stockings and bikini panties.

She caught his wrist, and a playful, arousing game of tug-of-war ensued beneath the linen table cloth. "Behave yourself," she murmured, her cheeks heating with a blush.

A sinful grin canted the corners of his mouth. "Now, what's the fun in that?" Withdrawing his hand, he winked at her, then turned his attention to his sister and brother-in-law. "Hey, Dean, how's the consultation work going?"

While other guests seated themselves and black-jacketed waiters circled the room to take drink orders from the tables, Natalie listened with interest as Dean and Noah discussed the free-lance business Dean had recently started. Since he'd been the CEO of a traffic-control business in Seattle before selling his company, he now offered his expertise to construction firms with bids and estimates on high-dollar projects. Natalie was amused to discover that Dean also accompanied his wife on the occasional bail-recovery assignment she took on through the investigative agency.

As the conversation continued between couples and the band struck up some light dinner music, Jennifer was passed around the table to familiar faces to keep her amused and occupied. When it came to Noah's turn to take her, he did so without hesitating, his big hands easily fitting around her little waist.

He held her up in the air and wiggled her until she gave him a big, toothless smile. "How's my favorite niece?" he said, his tone deep, but infinitely gentle.

"She's your *only* niece, Noah," Jo said wryly, pointing out the obvious.

"Which makes her my favorite," he said, never taking his gaze from the little girl in his arms. "Isn't that right, princess?" He blew a raspberry on her neck, making her squeal with delight and clasp his cheeks in her hands.

Natalie laughed as Jennifer tugged at his bow tie and grabbed at the flower on his lapel, and Noah fended off each of her attempts with a tickle or something equally distracting. And when she drooled on his crisp white dress shirt he didn't so much as blink twice.

Natalie didn't know, or perhaps didn't remember, that he had a such a soft spot for kids, but there was no denying how full her heart felt at the sight of Noah with the baby girl, and just how comfortable he was playing with her. The man would make a great father one day, and the thought made her own stomach flutter at the notion of being the one to carry his child.

The salads arrived, followed by dinner, then pure celebration took precedence for the rest of the evening, along with traditional wedding customs. The bride and groom shared the first dance, then cut the big, elaborate four-tiered cake, which was then served to the guests.

Melodie tossed her bridal bouquet to the small group of unmarried women, and while Natalie had joined in on the festivity with Joelle urging her on, she'd never expected to be the one to catch the bundle of flowers. She stood off to the side, and no one was more surprised than her when the bouquet hit her in the chest and dropped right into the hands she automatic shot out in front of her to protect herself from the floral slingshot.

She was rewarded with cheers and congratulations, and her gaze sought out Noah, who was watching her with a smile. Their connection was intimate and soulful, but she detected a deeper reserve about him, as if the fact that she held the flowers in her hand was a trick of some kind. Yet they were engaged, which meant there was just as much reality attached to the tradition as wishful thinking.

As the single men gathered out on the dance floor,

Cole removed the garter from his wife's leg and shot it out to the crowd of bachelors. Aggressive and competitive, Noah jumped high to snatch the garter out of the air and claim it for his own. The men around him clapped him on the back, seemingly grateful that they weren't next in line to slip on the old ball and chain. When Noah started toward her with his prize in hand and a predatory, determined light in his eyes, excitement took hold.

Without warning or hesitation, he wrapped a strong arm around her waist, hauled her close and kissed her, staking a claim on her in front of family and friends in a way no one could misinterpret.

She was his.

By the time he lifted his head and grinned down at her, she was completely breathless, aroused and flushed from his very public display. As she met Noah's tender, affectionate gaze, her heart swelled with love for him, so full it felt near to bursting with emotion.

And for the moment, for the night, the feelings between them were all that mattered to her.

By ELEVEN THAT NIGHT, the wedding revelry had died down considerably, leaving the last of the die-hard party guests to bring the evening's celebration to a close. A couple of dozen people remained, milling around and conversing with friends, and taking advantage of the music the band was still playing.

Since Cole and Melodie had slipped out of the reception an hour earlier to get a head start on their wedding night, Noah had taken it upon himself to issue goodbyes and thank-yous to the guests as they left the dwindling party.

After bidding Melodie's father and his date a good-night, Noah headed back inside the ballroom to see how Natalie was holding up and if she was ready to go, too. It had been a busy day and evening for both of them. From across the room he spotted her sitting at their table with no other adult company. His breath caught, and his heart seemed to lodge in his throat at the sight that greeted him.

Wearing that sexy dress with her hair in a fancy knot atop her head, Natalie was beautiful enough to stop him in his tracks. But it was the picture of her holding a sleeping Jennifer snuggled in the crook of her arm that gave him a jolt he felt all the way to the depths of his soul. Natalie's expression was serene as she gazed at the baby girl, her features reflecting awe and contentment.

And that sense of security and peace would soon be shattered, he knew. Maybe not tonight, but there was a man out there determined to wreak havoc on Natalie's life, who would also put in jeopardy the tenuous relationship they'd forged. Sooner or later, the truth *would* be revealed.

Pushing the disturbing thought aside, he strolled across the room to Natalie. He sat down in the chair next to her, and she looked up at him with a soft smile.

"I see you got roped into baby-sitting," he commented, amazed that the baby could sleep through the loud music blaring out of the speakers.

"I offered my services." She glanced down and drifted her fingers over the soft tufts of blond hair on the little girl's head in a loving gesture. "Jennifer was getting fussy and I thought I'd give Jo and Dean a break so they could enjoy a few dances without worrying about the baby."

"That was nice of you." Then again, he wasn't surprised. The woman had a generous, giving heart.

She shrugged. "Considering the very busy day she had, all it took was a few sips of milk from her bottle and she was out like a light."

Noah highly suspected that Natalie's maternal instincts had a lot to do with why his niece was cuddled so trustingly in her arms, as well. He experienced a twinge of envy as he took in the way Jennifer's cheek was pressed to Natalie's soft breast. He knew from personal experience just how comfortable those twin pillows could be.

He looked out toward the dance floor, finding his sister and brother-in-law enjoying the tunes being played. Jo was obviously teasing Dean over something that made the other man unexpectedly grab her around the waist and twirl her around in a series of fancy dance moves, which made Jo laugh out loud. Her blue eyes sparkled, and Noah loved seeing his sister so happy, and no longer allowing past mistakes to dictate her future. Both Noah and Cole had Dean to thank for Jo's transformation, and considered him as much a part of the family as another sibling.

"Jo and Dean seem to be having a good time," he said, speaking what was on his mind.

"Hmm, so am I," Natalie replied, her gaze never leaving the baby in her arms. She pressed a finger against Jennifer's tiny palm and the little girl instinctively clutched Natalie's finger in her sleep. Natalie sighed, the sound rife with longing. "Isn't she just the sweetest thing you've ever seen?"

Leaning close, Noah nuzzled Natalie's neck, inhaling deeply of her warm, feminine fragrance tinged with the scent of baby powder. "After you, yes."

She shivered and cast him a look filled with sensual promise...for later. "You know how to say all the right things, don't you."

He grinned rakishly. "I speak the truth."

She rolled her eyes and returned her gaze to Jennifer. "Just look at her, Noah. She's so perfect."

"That's because she's sleeping," he said, a teasing inflection in his tone. "You obviously haven't been on the receiving end of her crankiness. Jen takes after her mother. When she's in one of those moods she reminds me of Jo when she's ticked off." He shuddered for effect.

Soft laughter escaped Natalie. "You are *so* bad." She met his gaze, suddenly growing serious. "Holding her in my arms, I realize that I want a big family someday, especially since I was an only child and didn't have any siblings. I want that, for me and our children."

Our children. Oh, wow. Her reference to them having babies together struck him square in the chest, toppling him a bit off balance emotionally. He wanted things with Natalie that he'd never dreamed possible, never allowed himself to believe could be his. A wife. Babies. A family of his very own. It all seemed so close, so within his reach…yet they were living a lie, and their relationship was still precarious at best.

"What about you, Noah?" she asked, her question definitely calling for an answer, especially since she believed they were engaged to be married and a discussion about kids would be perfectly normal. "Do you want a big family?"

He swallowed hard and dredged up the most honest response he could put together. "Yeah, when the time is right, I would love a big family."

She gave him a soft, lingering kiss on his lips. "I'm glad we agree on that."

Minutes later, Jo and Dean came up to the table, breathless and looking like newlyweds themselves, and Noah was grateful for the interruption, which distracted Natalie from more talk about babies.

"I think us old married folk are going to head home and put the little one to bed," Dean said.

Noah witnessed a shared look between the couple, and saw Dean's excuse for what it was…the chance to spend a romantic evening with his wife. Noah understood, because he couldn't wait to get Natalie alone, either.

Natalie brushed her lips over Jennifer's brow, then glanced up at Jo. "If you ever need a baby-sitter, just let me know. I absolutely adore her."

"Thank you for the offer. And judging by how content she looks, I think the adoration is mutual."

Dean gathered up his sleeping daughter while Jo collected the baby paraphernalia on the table and dumped it into the diaper bag. With one last goodbye, the trio exited the party, leaving Noah and Natalie sitting alone at their table.

Just as the band switched to a slow ballad, Noah picked up Natalie's hand and caressed his thumb over her knuckles. "How about one last slow dance before we head home, too?"

She nodded and stood. "I would love that."

He led her out to the parquet floor where only a handful of other couples were enjoying the music, and pulled her tight into his embrace. She wrapped her arms around his neck and flowed into him, breasts to chest, thighs to thighs. He splayed a hand at the small of her back and aligned their hips, too. Their bodies brushed with every movement, heightening the awareness between them.

Natalie looked up at him, her gaze searching his in the dim lighting. "Noah...when are we getting married?"

Her unexpected question startled him for a moment. Then frustration settled in. It was getting more and more difficult to keep up the pretense between them, to continue to let Natalie believe something that just wasn't real, no matter how much Noah wished otherwise. "We haven't set a date yet."

"Maybe we should," she said, smoothing her hand beneath his suit jacket, her palm coming to rest over his rapidly beating heart. "That way I can have something to look forward to and start planning."

He hated denying her anything, but refused to put such a life-altering change into motion when their engagement was based on fabrications. And more and more he wanted their relationship based on reality, truth and trust. "When your memory returns we'll talk about it," he said, giving her at least that much. "I promise."

She released a soft sound teeming with impatience. "There you go again, coddling me."

He allowed a slight smile to make an appearance. "I'm not coddling you. I just think that discussing a wedding date isn't as important as making sure you're better and your memory is back to normal."

It was obvious by her determined expression that she disagreed. "All right," she finally relented. "But just for the record, I don't have to like your way of thinking."

He chuckled at her bit of defiance and tucked her head against his chest. "I didn't expect you to, sweetheart."

As the music played, she softened against him, as much a part of him as the steady beat of his heart. And that's when he knew that he couldn't go on like this, deceiving her with their relationship, playing with her emotions. The complete truth had to be told, their circumstances and feigned engagement explained, even at the risk of losing her.

But first he wanted one last night with her.

10

LESS THAN AN HOUR LATER, Noah shrugged out of his formal jacket, tossed it onto the chair in the corner of his bedroom and locked gazes with the woman who made him hard with wanting. "Have I told you how incredibly sexy you look in that dress you're wearing?"

With a sensual smile curving her lips, she closed the distance between them, tugged his bow tie loose and dropped it to the floor. Then she started in on the buttons of his dress shirt, her warm lips kissing each inch of skin she bared. "Yeah, you have, and I do believe you made mention of wondering what I'm wearing beneath it, too."

"So I did," he said huskily, helping her as she pushed his shirt off his shoulders, down his arms and off. "Is that an invitation to find out?"

Laving one of his nipples with the flat of her tongue, she unbuckled his belt, pulled his zipper carefully over his enormous erection, and let his trousers fall to pool around his bare feet. His briefs followed, which he promptly kicked aside, leaving him completely naked while she remained fully dressed.

"Consider it an invitation, a dare, a challenge."

She knelt in front of him, her palms sliding down his hair-roughened thighs as she went. "I'm game for any or all three."

He chuckled at her playful reply, then groaned as she wrapped her fingers around his aching shaft and stroked him from base to tip, drawing a bead of clear fluid from the head of his penis. Pulling the clip from her hair, he tangled his fingers in the spill of silky strands and *dared* her to indulge in a more carnal intimacy.

He watched his fantasy unfold as her lashes drifted shut, her lips parted, and she enveloped him in the wet heat and suction of her mouth. She teased him with her tongue, drawing him deeper still, and when she moaned in the back of her throat, the sound vibrated along his shaft and threatened his control.

Effortlessly, she'd taken over the reins of tonight's seduction. She pushed him to the brink, testing his restraint not once, but twice, before she finally stopped, leaving him full and throbbing for release. Refusing to go there without her along for the ride, he pulled her back up and captured her mouth with his, taking over with a challenge of his own.

Their tongues tangled and mated as he tugged the sleeves of her dress all the way down her arms. With a helpful shimmy of her hips, the sweater material slid the rest of the way off her body. When he finally stepped back and looked his fill of her, standing there in a strapless bra, barely there string-bikini panties and silky thigh-high stockings, the first thought that filled his mind was that she was a sexy centerfold come to life. His own personal playmate to enjoy and devour.

''This was definitely worth waiting for,'' he murmured appreciatively.

Dipping his head, he traced the full swells of her lush breasts with his tongue while reaching behind her to release the catch on her bra. The garment fell to the floor, and he latched onto a taut nipple, suckling her as his name tumbled from her lips. He cupped her other breast in his palm, fondling the warm, resilient flesh until the dual assault had her body twisting against him and her fingers digging into the muscles of his back.

He straightened, and with a hot, deep kiss he guided her back toward the foot of the bed and onto the center of the mattress. He didn't join her just yet, too enthralled by the sight of her lying there. Her blond hair haloed her head, her breasts rose and fell with each deep breath she took, those insubstantial panties covered her feminine secrets, and the provocative stockings encased her long, slender limbs.

Hooking his fingers beneath the thin strings at the sides of her panties, he dragged the damp scrap of fabric down her legs while his lips pressed hot, moist, openmouthed kisses up her thighs. His tongue tasted, his teeth marked her, and she writhed and moaned under his ministrations.

Once her underwear was off, she automatically opened her stocking-clad legs, issuing him the final invitation to come inside her. He did, using his tongue and fingers to make love to her and take her to the edge of orgasm. Again and again, he teased and tormented her with the promise of an explosive climax, just as she'd done to him.

When he was confident that she was primed for him and a few strokes away from release, he rolled on a condom and knelt between her legs. But instead of driving into her as she seemed to expect, he shoved a pillow beneath her bottom, raising her pelvis higher, and draped her thighs over his so that his pulsing cock nestled against the warmth and dewy wetness of her sex.

She looked up at him, a sultry smile on her lips. "You have a thing for pillows, don't you."

"It gives me better leverage, and deeper access." His hand smoothed down her flat belly and his thumb pressed against her swollen clitoris, making her groan and grip the covers at her sides. "Do you mind?"

"Not at all. I'm all yours, to do with as you please." She dampened her bottom lip with her tongue and asked, "Aren't you going to take off my stockings?"

"No, I don't think I am." His other hand trailed over the strip of bare skin where the lacy bands of her stockings ended, and his stomach muscles constricted in restraint. "I find the contrast of sheer black nylon against your pale, creamy flesh highly erotic."

She blinked lazily, sensually. "You make me feel erotic."

Aching to be inside her, he guided the head of his shaft between her slick folds, found her opening and pushed forward, watching as she took the entire length of him. She made a small sound of pleasure as he buried himself to the hilt, though he didn't move or thrust, just savored the heat and tightness and wonder of being such an intimate part of her.

Keeping his finger on that pulsing nub of flesh at the hood of her sex, he lifted his gaze to hers. Now that he was inside her, he didn't want their lovemaking to end, though he knew it was inevitable. But before he sent them both soaring, he needed to know what was going through her mind, what was happening in her heart.

"What else do I make you feel?" he murmured, arousing her all over again with the slow, slick slide of his fingers.

"Desired," she whispered breathlessly, moving against him in an instinctive motion that drew him deeper. "And cherished."

Unable to hold off any longer, done tormenting them both, he gave her body what it craved, using a firm, seductive touch to make her unravel. He watched her beautiful expression as she came, savoring her soft cries of completion, determined to devote everything about this passionate moment, this woman, to memory, and praying she did the same.

Before the contractions ebbed completely, he moved over her, pressing her deeper into the mattress with the weight of his body, and the heavy, rhythmic glide of his thrusts. He entwined their fingers at the side of her head and she locked her heels at the base of his spine, the tilted angle of her hips granting him deeper penetration and greater friction.

She gasped as he pumped harder, higher, and he watched ecstasy play across her features as yet another orgasm convulsed through her. She quivered beneath him, her inner muscles tightening around his length, milking him with exquisite spasms and coaxing him over that razor-sharp edge of pleasure with her. Arching into her one last time, he tossed his head back with a low, primal growl and gave himself over to the branding heat and scorching climax that jolted down his spine and rocketed through his veins.

Utterly drained, he lowered himself fully on top of her, heartbeat to heartbeat, and kissed her tenderly, deeply, loathe to separate their bodies and shatter the cocoon of intimacy that was theirs alone to share. Possibly, for the very last time.

Minutes later, he lifted his head and smoothed her hair away from her face. "Are you okay?"

A soft smile curved her lips. "Mmm, never better." Her fingers touched his jaw, his lips, and she suddenly grew very serious. "I love you," she whispered, the truth of her emotions shining bright in her eyes, along with a wealth of trust that he didn't deserve. "I just needed to say the words out loud."

His chest tightened in response, and he swallowed hard. "I love you, too," he said, unable to deny what was in his own heart, as well.

She brought his mouth back to hers, sealing the profound moment with a slow, languid kiss that made both of their bodies quicken with renewed desire. And as Noah proceeded to make love to her again, he couldn't help but wonder what this night, and their declarations, would cost them both come the morning when he revealed the truth.

NOAH HAD NEVER BEEN SO afraid of losing anything in his entire life. From a very early age he'd learned to guard his thoughts and feelings, protect his emotions from potential pain, and form no attachments other than to his immediate family.

He'd broken every single one of those rules with Natalie, who'd gotten under his skin and filled an emptiness in him he hadn't even known existed until her. And for the first time ever, he wanted a woman in his life permanently, was willing to risk everything to give up his solitary lifestyle and make a forever kind of commitment to Natalie, who was just as much of a lost and lonely soul as he'd been.

But first the truth between them beckoned.

Uncertainties and doubts attacked Noah's empty stomach, invading his system like angry bees, making him all too aware of everything Natalie stood to lose, too. Inhaling a steady breath, he squeezed his eyes shut, dipped his head beneath the hot, harsh spray of water in the shower, and tried to wash away his misgivings about their upcoming conversation.

She'd told him she loved him, and while last night he'd rejoiced in the declaration, now a small, insecure part of him couldn't stop analyzing her revelation. Did she truly love him, or did she only *believe* she loved him because of her amnesia and their intimate situation?

He was so damned torn and confused, he couldn't

think straight. He craved time and distance to clear his head and figure out the best way to tell her the truth—that their relationship was all a fabrication that started out as a way to protect her, and ended up with him so emotionally involved he knew he'd never be the same again. No matter the outcome of their discussion.

Shutting off the shower, he dried off with a towel and quietly got dressed in jeans and a T-shirt, then socks and sneakers. He walked over to the bed where Natalie was still sleeping and took in her disheveled hair and content expression, knowing he was responsible for both. He leaned down and brushed a soft kiss across her cheek, watching as she blinked her eyes open and looked up at him with a frown.

"What are you doing out of bed and dressed?" she asked, her disappointment plain.

"It's nine-thirty, sleepyhead," he said with a smile. "Do you plan on staying in bed all day long?"

"Maybe, if you'll consider joining me." Grinning shamelessly, she stretched her lithe body, uncaring of the covers that fell to her waist and revealed her naked breasts.

It took every ounce of control he possessed to resist her very tempting offer to spend the day in bed with her and forget about the real world. He straightened and thrust his fingers into the front pockets of his jeans to keep from touching her warm, supple skin and luscious curves. "How about I go out and get us some pastries and lattes for breakfast?"

"Mmm," she said, the one word a provocative, come-hither purr in her throat. "I could handle that."

"Great." He took a step back, then another, fighting his body's desires with the need to make things right with her before they made love again. "I'll be back in about half an hour," he promised, and then he was gone.

NATALIE LAY IN BED, listening to the sound of Noah's light footsteps heading down the stairs to the foyer. She heard him stop there to set the silent house alarm before leaving to pick up breakfast. A small smile touched her lips at his protective nature, though now that she knew why he was taking extra precautions with her safety, she appreciated his attentiveness.

She heard his car back out of the driveway, then an overwhelming silence settled over the house, along with the realization that she didn't like being alone. After a week of constantly being surrounded by people, she felt a bit uneasy being companionless. Which was ridiculous, she knew, since she clearly couldn't spend the rest of her life with a bodyguard attached to her side.

Yet it seemed by Noah's reserved behavior this morning and his restless desire to get out of the house that he needed a reprieve, even if it was a brief one. In a way she understood. Last night had been so emotionally intense, a surrender of hearts and souls in a way that felt like the very first time for her. She'd been thrown by the depth of her feelings for Noah and hadn't been able to hold back the declaration that had felt so perfectly right.

Yet for as much as he'd returned her sentiment, there had been a few times she'd sensed uncertainties within him, as if something deep and personal was going on in his mind that he wasn't ready or willing to divulge just yet. Then again, there was always the possibility that she might be reading too much into her own insecurities.

With a sigh, she got out of bed and padded to the bathroom. After taking care of personal business, she brushed her teeth and changed into her drawstring pants and a loose, comfy T-shirt. Just as she finished combing out the tangles in her hair, the sound of shattering glass downstairs made her jump, and her heart accelerated to a hard, pounding beat.

Startled, and certain Noah had returned and accidentally broken something, she dropped the brush on the vanity and started out of the bedroom and down the stairs.

"Noah?" she called, and came to an abrupt halt when she saw that the glass from one of the windows flanking the front door was scattered on the floor in the entryway. The door was ajar, and the morning breeze wafted indoors. The cool air caused goose bumps to rise on her flesh, contradicting the hot prickle of unease invading her entire body.

Her gaze shot to the security system on the wall. The red light on the alarm panel flashed, indicating the silent alarm had been set off. Noah wasn't home, and someone had obviously broken into the house.

The phone rang, the loud, jangling noise breaking through the silence and Natalie's paralyzed nerves. Praying it was Noah, or even the security company, she leapt over the shattered glass on the floor, ran into the kitchen and grabbed the portable unit. Before she could connect the call a familiar male figure appeared on the other side of the counter and ripped the phone line from the wall, leaving her with a dead unit in her hand.

She screamed in fright and stumbled back a few steps. Terror gripped her as she stared at the man who'd been stalking her—her ex-boyfriend, according to Noah. A man who obviously had no qualms about breaking and entering to get what he wanted. And what he wanted was *her*.

Oh, God.

An arrogant smile lifted his lips. "Hello, Natalie," he said, though he didn't make any move toward her. The counter between the family room and kitchen still separated them, but his presence emanated an underlying animosity she felt to her bones.

Shaking from the inside out, she curled her fingers tight around the receiver in her hand to keep her grounded. "Ch-Ch-Chad," she stammered, surprised that her vocal chords worked.

He lifted a blond brow, looking immensely pleased at her recollection. "You finally remember me. I was beginning to think that your amnesia, and Noah's influence on you, had permanently erased me from your memory."

His voice was low and tinged with malevolence.

Disjointed memories flashed in her mind, of Chad's face twisted with fury and a temper to match. And then the recollection crystallized. She'd been the victim of that rage before—it was what had caused her to leave Chad and start a new life here in Oakland.

She was stunned by the memory, and terrified by Chad's irrational frame of mind and what he was capable of doing to her. "Get out, *now,*" she ordered adamantly.

"We'll be leaving together this time," he said, too calmly. "Do you know how long I've been waiting to catch you alone? It hasn't been easy with your watchdog by your side at all times."

Refusing to turn her back on him, she took a step back, then another, edging closer to her only means of escape—a framed threshold leading to the formal dining room and the stairs that headed up to the second level of the house. She thought of Noah's revolver in the bedroom upstairs, and knew that it was her best source of defense against this deranged man.

But she had to get to the weapon first.

"You'll always be mine, Natalie," Chad said possessively, drawing her full attention back to him.

Her chest tightened as his familiar words sank in. They were the same as the words she'd read on the card that had accompanied the bouquet she'd received at the hospital. Noah hadn't sent her those flowers, she realized. Chad had.

"You never should have left me," he chided as he moved around the counter, his steps deceptively slow and unhurried, his gaze dark and direct. "Did you really think that I wouldn't be able to find you? And I can't believe that your lover thought that I couldn't get to you, just because you were locked in his house. You're *mine,* and this time I'm not letting you go.''

He was too close, too dangerous, and she'd had enough. Taking advantage of the only weapon and distraction she had available to her, she pitched the phone in her hand at Chad's head. The unit hit its mark, striking him in the temple. He grabbed his head and howled in pain, and she turned and ran through the opposite doorway and up the stairs, desperate to get to Noah's gun.

Once she'd made it to the master bedroom, she shut and locked the door. She bolted over to the dresser and rummaged through the drawer where he kept his revolver, her heart beating in time with the heavy, angry footsteps of Chad coming up the stairs.

She tossed Noah's cotton undershirts onto the floor in her frantic search, and a sob of despair caught in her throat when she realized that the gun was gone. He must have donned it this morning, though for the life of her she couldn't remember him wearing his holster, which didn't mean much. She'd grown so used to the weapon being a part of him that she hardly noticed it anymore.

But the fact remained that the gun was gone, and she was trapped upstairs with a crazed man after her.

The bedroom door rattled as Chad tried to kick in the sturdy wooden panel, spurring Natalie to find another means of defense. She'd gone through two other drawers for something sharp or blunt to use when the door cracked and splintered from the force of Chad's repeated blows, then crashed open.

She jumped back with a gasp, while he stood there in the doorway, the cut near his temple oozing blood down the side of his face. His features were filled with violent rage.

Fear swelled within her. "I'm expecting Noah back any minute," she blurted out, hoping and praying it was true. "I suggest you leave before he returns."

Chad strolled into the room, seemingly unfazed by her threat. "Ahh, Noah, your *fiancé,*" he drawled in a chilly tone, and smirked. "Do you really believe that lie he told you?"

She shook her head in confusion as she backed toward the far side of the room to keep distance between them. Knowing conversation was her best stall tactic until she could figure out an escape, she asked, "What lie?"

"The two of you aren't engaged." He waved an impatient hand in the air. "I've been watching you long enough to know that the two of you weren't *ever* an item, at least not before the night of your accident."

His comment rippled through her mind, and denial rose fast and furiously. Of course she and Noah were engaged! They lived together. She'd given him her body, her soul. *She loved him.*

But along with that denial came snippets of conversations she'd had with Noah, of him skirting the issue of their engagement, no ring on her finger, no wedding date set, and no straightforward answers to the many questions she'd asked about them as a couple.

More vague images appeared in her head...Noah at the bar, talking and flirting with her, walking out with her the night of the accident, and her playfully fending off his flirtatious advances. They'd been friends, acquaintances, nothing more. The memories were fresh and real and gave her no choice but to believe Chad's words.

She and Noah weren't engaged.

The truth crashed over her in waves, shaking the very foundation of her relationship with Noah, which in essence had been nothing more than an affair. No wonder so much hadn't made sense to her.

"I thought you'd finally changed," Chad went on bitterly, touching her personal items on the dresser, taking a whiff from her perfume bottle before continuing toward her. "But being the slut that you are, you moved in with him, slept with him and now you're his *whore.*"

Whore. She winced, remembering Chad cursing her with that exact word the night he'd attacked her after work in Reno.

He'd claimed she was a tramp for using her body as a showgirl, and he didn't like other men looking at her, lusting after her. Memories of her tumultuous past with Chad deluged her mind, overwhelming her—memories she would have been happy to keep suppressed. But this confrontation triggered a release of recollections she couldn't stop or escape.

Swallowing the whimper of panic rising to the surface, she kept inching backward, until her spine pressed up against the wall and she found herself cornered by Chad and the king-size bed to her left.

Knowing she was trapped, Chad continued to approach her like a savage animal anticipating pouncing on his prey. "I've had enough of watching you with him. Now I'm going to take back what's mine."

Her chance of escape was slim, but she wasn't going to let Chad bully her anymore. She refused to be a victim any longer, refused to allow this man any power over her mind or body—as he'd had in her past.

Resolute and more determined than she'd ever been before, she sprinted to the left and dove for the bed so she could scramble across the mattress. She made it halfway across before she felt a large hand clamp around her ankle and yank her back. She flipped over just as Chad started to move on top of her, his intent clear.

He was going to assault her.

And she was going to fight for her life, without remorse or hesitation. Just as he let go of her ankle, she kicked, *hard,* and aimed high. Her foot connected with his jaw with a loud crack, and his head snapped back from the impact. Her other foot landed in the middle of his chest, knocking him off balance and giving her the reprieve she needed to get the hell away from him.

"Goddamn whore!" he bellowed furiously, the agony of her dual attack radiating in his eyes.

She rolled away from him and off the bed. As soon

as her feet hit the floor she was running out the door and down the stairs. He was seconds behind her, cursing her and promising retribution every step of the way. Before she could reach the foyer and front door, shards of glass be damned, he grabbed a handful of her hair and pulled her to an abrupt stop.

She yelped in pain but didn't stop moving, her arms swinging, hands punching, and legs and feet striking any body part she came in contact with. They stumbled into the living room, and she kicked him in the shin, expecting his instant reflexes to cause him to let her go.

No such luck. Another explicit curse filled the air and he shoved her down onto the floor between the couch and coffee table, pinning her there with the weight of his body. He straddled her thighs, taking away any chance she might have had to knee him in the groin.

She wanted to scream in frustration but didn't waste her energy on something that would be of no help to her predicament.

He stared down at her, his nostrils flaring with each labored breath he took. "I'm going to take what's mine. Right here. Right now."

"Go to hell," she said through gritted teeth. "You're nothing but a hypocrite! You call me a whore, yet you have no qualms about using my body to slake *your* lust!"

He clenched his swollen jaw and narrowed his gaze to tiny slits. "It doesn't matter. You're used goods, anyway."

Grabbing the neckline of her shirt, he ripped it right down the middle, exposing her breasts encased in a thin cotton bra. She fought to fend him off, then ceased her struggles when she caught sight of the bronze statue on the coffee table next to her. As much as it revolted her, she let his hands grope her and didn't issue a protest when his mouth touched down on the upper slope of one breast.

Swallowing the nausea rolling in her belly, she sank her fingers into his hair in the pretense of enjoying his kisses, feigned a sigh of surrender and reached for the bronze statue. As soon as her fingers curled around the cool metal she jerked Chad's head back and bashed the statue against the side of his head. The first hit merely dazed him. The second strike rendered him unconscious.

He slumped on top of her, and with a deep sob she immediately shoved him off and crawled away from his lifeless form, the statue still clutched in her hand. She pressed her back up against the wall just as the sound of a vehicle skidded to a stop in the driveway. Seconds later, two uniformed police officers charged into the house, guns drawn—no doubt sent by the security company when she hadn't answered the phone.

They took one look at her ripped shirt and devastated expression, coupled with the man crumpled on the floor, and came to all the right conclusions. They made sure she was physically unharmed, then proceeded to take care of Chad, locking him in cuffs and rendering him immobile so he'd be no threat when he gained consciousness.

As they called for backup and an ambulance for Chad, Natalie buried her face in her hands. She finally broke down, allowing her emotions and tears to flow freely and releasing the fear, anxiety and pain she'd kept bottled up inside of her for too long.

But mostly, she wept for the empty future without Noah that awaited her after today. She understood now that their relationship had been based on a lie, a fabrication she'd fallen for, deeply and irrevocably, when in reality she'd been merely a responsibility for Noah. He'd taken her into his home to protect her from Chad since she couldn't recall her past, and she'd fallen for the protective ruse. But Noah had never truly been hers. Their relationship, his family, the sense of belonging she'd experienced...it had all been a false sense of security that had now been shattered by the return of her memory.

Despite his tale that they were engaged, she couldn't blame Noah for the affair they'd had, since she'd been the one to allow her own suppressed needs and desires to blossom and take flight. She'd tempted and teased him, instigating those first few erotic encounters and ultimately seducing him into making love to her.

She'd just had no idea how intimately involved her heart, body and soul would become with Noah—in a way she'd never given to another man. And while she harbored no regrets for loving him, neither did she expect him to make her promises of forever. As she now remembered, he'd been a confirmed bachelor before her memory loss, a man who enjoyed his freedom and carefree, uncomplicated lifestyle.

And she was a woman who'd never let a man as close as she'd allowed Noah, for fear of losing her sense of self, as she almost had with Chad. The amnesia had loosened her inhibitions and left her much too vulnerable to love. To Noah.

She swiped at the moisture beneath her eyes and on her cheeks and shored up her resolve. With her memory back and the crisis of being stalked over, it was time for her to move on and start out fresh—no matter how much she dreaded a life without Noah.

11

THE MOMENT NOAH PULLED INTO his driveway and saw a patrol car and ambulance parked in front of his house, fear nearly strangled him. He jumped out of his vehicle and ran.

The broken window next to the front door and the shards of glass crunching beneath his sneakered feet as he bolted into the foyer sickened him, adding to his anxiety and dread that Chad had finally gotten to Natalie.

In his living room, he came across the paramedics strapping Chad to a cot, and Noah's stomach lurched when he caught sight of the blood on the other man's face, and his lifeless form. His gaze frantically swept the general area for Natalie, and his chest tightened with apprehension when he didn't find her.

Where in the hell was she? Had they already taken her away in a separate ambulance? Or, God forbid, had she been fatally hurt?

Desperate to know *something* before he went insane with worry, he grabbed the arm of a passing EMT, and the young man looked up at him in startled surprise. Now that Noah had the technician's attention, he released him.

"Where's the woman?" he asked, his voice hoarse.

The man hooked a finger toward the adjoining room. "She's in the kitchen with the police."

"Thank you," he muttered, and strode into the kitchen, instantly finding her sitting at the table in the corner nook with two police officers taking her statement. Relief at seeing her alive mingled with a stabbing pain in the vicinity of Noah's heart as he took in her disheveled hair, puffy eyes and the dried tears streaking her cheeks. Her shirt was torn, and she was holding it together with one hand.

Guilt swamped him, making him weak in the knees. She'd been attacked, and he hadn't been there to protect her. The realization hit him like a swift punch to his gut. He knew what Chad was capable of and had sworn to keep Natalie safe, yet he'd left her alone and vulnerable to the other man.

Would she ever forgive him for being so careless with her life?

Natalie glanced beyond the police officers in front of her, her eyes widening when she saw him standing there. Both men followed her line of vision, and perceiving Noah as a threat, they placed a hand on their holstered weapons and narrowed their shrewd gazes on him.

"Who are *you?*" one of the blue-uniformed men asked.

Noah raised his hands, making sure that the officers saw that he was carrying a revolver beneath his untucked shirt so it didn't come as a surprise to them later. "I'm the owner of the house, and Natalie is my fiancée."

"Are you licensed to carry a concealed weapon?" the other officer demanded.

"Yes, sir." Very slowly, Noah withdrew his wallet, showing the men his identification and his P.I. badge. "Can I have a few moments alone with her, please?"

Still skeptical, one of the officers asked Natalie, "Do you know him, ma'am?"

She nodded jerkily, apparently still in shock from all that had happened. "Yes, I do. I'll be fine with him."

As soon as the two men exited the kitchen, Noah pulled Natalie up from the chair and wrapped her in his arms. He felt the steady beat of her heart against his chest and absorbed the warmth of her body, the scent of her skin. Then he pulled back and searched her face, needing confirmation that she was unharmed, despite the harrowing way things looked.

"Did Chad hurt you in any way?" he asked, his muscles tensing at the possibility.

"Mostly, he just scared me," she said softly, and managed a slight smile, though her body language was too guarded with him compared to her open, candid personality of the past week.

She sat back down and smoothed her tousled hair away from her face. "Did you happen to get a look at Chad?" she asked, a teasing inflection in her tone. "He's in worse shape than I am."

He heard the pride in her voice, that she'd fought

Chad and won the battle. But where did that leave *them?* The emotional distance he felt growing between them frustrated him, and he hoped her reserve was because of the recent trauma she'd suffered, and not because she was withdrawing from him.

"Yeah, I saw Chad." He took the chair next to hers. Desperate for some kind of connection to her, he reached for her slender hand and pressed it between his palms. "Can you tell me what happened?" He needed to know what she'd gone through, if she was truly all right—mentally, emotionally and physically.

She inhaled a deep breath, but didn't back down from reliving the nightmare she'd just endured. "He broke in right after you left and tried to attack me," she began, and filled him in on all the details, right up to the point where Chad had pinned her to the living room floor with the intention of raping her. "When I saw your bronze statue on the coffee table, I knew it was my last chance, so I used it to knock him out cold."

Noah grinned as he kissed the tips of her fingers, amazed at her tenacity. "You are so incredibly brave, and I'm so proud of you."

Her chin lifted stubbornly, her internal strength shining through. "I wasn't about to let him get away with terrorizing me this time."

"This time?" he echoed, catching her deliberate choice of words. "You remember your past with him?"

"Bits and pieces came back to me," she said, and

shuddered delicately. "Enough for me to recall that he'd had control over me in the past, that he'd been possessive and jealous to the point of being smothering."

He wondered what else she recollected during the course of the attack. He rolled his shoulders, which did nothing to ease the tension bunching his muscles. "I'm so sorry, Natalie," he said, his sincere apology a heartfelt plea for her forgiveness.

Her gaze met his steadily, her irises a stunning shade of blue. "What for?"

Her question was too pointed, delving deeper than the surface reasons for his apology, as if she knew much more than she was letting on. There was a wealth of confessions he owed her, but he went with the most obvious reply. "I *never* should have left you alone."

"There's nothing to forgive." Her smile was sad as she touched her fingers to his cheek in a loving caress. "You can't protect me forever, Noah. Chad was intent on getting to me, and it was all a matter of time. If not today, then tomorrow, or next week, or next month. And there's no way you could have known that he'd break into the house."

Still, guilt ate at him, along with so many regrets. He'd let her down, and in turn had let himself down, as well.

"I'm just glad everything is finally over," she said with a sigh. "Now we can go back to living normal lives."

She was glad everything was over? Including

them? And what the hell did she mean by them going back to living normal lives—with or without each other? Doubts, uncertainties and old fears flared bright and hot within him, raising his anxiety a few notches.

She gently but firmly pulled her hand from his grasp. "By the way, you don't have to pretend anymore," she said quietly.

He stared at her beautiful features, his outward calm belying his inner turmoil. "What do you mean?" His voice was low and rough.

Her shoulder lifted in an attempt at a casual shrug. "About you being my fiancé, and us being engaged."

Unable to help himself, he winced. "Has *all* of your memory returned?"

"Enough to remember that you and I weren't in a relationship before the car accident," she replied, her cheeks coloring a light shade of pink. "Not an intimate one, anyway."

Anxious and jumpy at her revelation, he stood and paced the small area in the kitchen. Natalie wasn't angry, just resigned and accepting of the choices he'd made on her behalf. Choices that had made her intimately his, body and soul.

"I never should have touched you, or made love to you," he said, even as he knew he never could have resisted her. He'd tried, only to fail. He'd gotten inside her body, and she'd found her way into his heart.

"I didn't give you much choice in the matter,

Noah," she said wryly. "I wanted you, and I don't regret a thing about our affair."

So, she was going to chalk up their relationship as an erotic, illicit tryst. The thought made him want to haul her over his shoulder again, carry her up to his bedroom and make love to her until she admitted she couldn't live without him.

"Noah," she said, interrupting his thoughts and making him realize that she was standing, too. "Why didn't you tell me the truth about us?"

He released a long breath and explained. He owed her at least that. "It all started at the hospital, as a way for me to get into your room and get information from the doctor about your condition. Once I told him that you were my fiancée I gained access to your room, along with your prognosis. And from there, the fabrication snowballed. The doctor said it was best to let you remember things on your own, and then when I realized you were being stalked, it was the best way to keep you safe and in my care without you insisting you could handle things on your own…which you tried to do a few times, if I remember correctly."

She ducked her head sheepishly, obviously remembering the way she'd argued with him about going back to work and school. The woman was stubborn and independent—traits that both frustrated and aroused him.

Closing the distance between them, he tucked a finger beneath her chin and lifted her gaze back to his. "Except I didn't do a very good job of protecting you, did I?"

"I don't blame you for anything, Noah." She bit her bottom lip, her eyes shining with emotions he couldn't define. "If anything, I owe you for taking me in when I had no one else to take care of me. I couldn't have asked for a better bodyguard than you've been to me."

He clenched his jaw with irritation. He didn't want her damn gratitude, or have his role in her life reduced to guardian. He ached to tell her again that he loved her, but would she even believe him, or just assume it had all been part of the ruse of their intimate relationship? And what of her declaration spoken in the heat of passion last night? Were her feelings for him real, or just part of what she'd perceived to be true before she learned actual reality today?

He was terrified to find out. Terrified of having fallen in love with this woman, only to lose her.

"I think I've imposed long enough," she went on pragmatically, looking away so he couldn't gauge her expression. "And now that Chad is going to be prosecuted and behind bars, there's no reason for me to stay here with you. As soon as the police are done questioning me, I think I should leave and go back to my own place."

He shoved his fingers deep into the front pockets of his jeans and forced himself to ask, "Are you sure that's what you want?" He left the beginning or the end of their relationship in her hands. One word, yes or no, would seal their fates and futures. Together, or alone.

She hesitated, long enough to get his hopes up and

make him believe that she might have a change of mind...a change of heart. Then she squared her shoulders and met his gaze, tough and strong and courageous.

"It's what I think is best," she whispered, giving nothing away, "for the both of us."

DESPITE NATALIE'S REQUEST that they go their separate ways, Noah couldn't stay away from her. Client cases consumed his days, especially since Cole and Melodie were still on their honeymoon, but he spent his evenings at Murphy's, just to be near Natalie, no matter how awkward and reserved things were between them now.

During the course of the past few nights it had been Gina who'd served him and Bobby their drinks, while Natalie handled a different section of the lounge. The times he came face-to-face with Natalie their conversations were friendly and polite, and he could have sworn he'd seen longing darkening her gaze. Or maybe it was all wishful thinking on his part.

All she had to do was say the word and he was hers, but so far she'd held true to her resolve to return their relationship back to the status quo of acquaintances. And he knew he had no one to blame for her decision but himself. He'd made the choice to entangle her in a fabrication that had destroyed any chance they might have had of a future together.

"Hey, Noah, it's your shot," Bobby said, snapping him out of his depressing thoughts and back to the game of pool at hand. "You've got solids."

Noah gave the front of the establishment one last quick glance for Natalie, who hadn't yet started her shift though it was nearly 7:00 p.m. Gina was working part of the lounge, while another waitress who usually worked a different shift covered the other section of the bar. Blowing out a tight breath tinged with frustration, he returned his attention to the placement of the billiard balls on the table. He lined up his cue, made the shot and completely missed the pocket he was aiming for.

He swore beneath his breath, though he wasn't surprised that he'd missed his mark. His game sucked lately.

Bobby lifted an amused brow his way. "Are you sure you don't want to trade in that soda you're drinking for a beer to loosen you up a bit?"

A wry grin canted the corners of Noah's mouth. "I doubt a few beers will cure what ails me."

Bobby leaned against his cue stick and studied Noah for a long moment before coming to his own conclusion about his friend's mood. "Man, you're in way over your head with Natalie, aren't you?"

I love her. The inescapable thought came automatically, though Noah kept the private words to himself. Bobby didn't know the extent of his relationship with Natalie—the intimacy they'd shared and the emotional depths in which he'd plunged.

Gina made her way to the back of the establishment and breezed by their table. "Either of you need a refill?" she asked.

"I'm fine," Bobby said, then made his shot, sinking two striped balls into two separate pockets.

"I'm good, too," Noah added, then dredged up the one question he knew Gina could answer for him. "Is Natalie off tonight?"

Gina cleared a nearby table and wiped down the surface. "I guess you could say that," she murmured.

Noah frowned, sensing much more to Gina's comment. "What do you mean by that?"

She glanced at him, searching his expression, then shook her head. "You don't know, do you?"

Witnessing the rueful look in Gina's eyes, Noah's stomach twisted into a knot of apprehension. "Know what?"

Gina hesitated, then finally said, "Natalie turned in her resignation this afternoon."

"She quit?" he asked incredulously. *"Why?"*

Gina chewed on her bottom lip, as if uncertain she should divulge any more information. She must have seen his desperation, because she finally put him out of his misery. "She told Murphy that she's moving."

A fresh wave of panic reared inside of him. "To where?"

Genuine regret filled Gina's eyes. "I honestly don't know, Noah."

"Order up, Gina," Murphy called from the service area, and she gave Noah a soft "I'm sorry" before hurrying over to the bar to pick up her drinks and deliver them.

Noah scrubbed a hand along his taut jaw and stared at Bobby, as if he could make sense of what was happening. "Where in the hell would she move to?" *And why?* Was she putting even more distance between them, or escaping memories of Chad's attack? Or a combination of both?

"I have no idea what goes on in the minds of most women. Maybe you should ask Natalie for yourself," Bobby suggested pragmatically.

Did he even have the right to question her choices? Noah wondered. After all she'd been through, after all he'd put her through, didn't she deserve to make the kind of decisions she felt were the best for her future? Even if that meant he wasn't a part of it?

Bobby came up beside him and placed a hand on his shoulder. "Don't let her go without telling her how you really feel. If you don't at least try to bridge the gap between the two of you, you'll regret it for the rest of your life."

The profundity of his friend's words of wisdom made Noah curious. "Are you speaking from personal experience?"

Bobby shrugged, neither confirming or denying the direct question. "Just trust me on this, Noah. If she's the woman you love, then fight for her."

Noah had never been put in such a position before, having to win the affection of a woman. But then, he'd never wanted a woman as much as he needed Natalie in his life. And how ironic was it that he'd protected his emotions for so long, only to fall for the one woman who remained elusive to him?

He'd watched Joelle and Cole struggle with the same fears and doubts not that long ago. He'd even helped them to recognize the weaknesses that had prevented them from grasping happiness together. What

Noah hadn't admitted to himself was that he'd been afflicted with the same insecurities as a result of his shaky childhood.

The scared little boy in him who'd faced so much rejection and pain in the past had kept him from laying his soul on the line the morning Chad had attacked Natalie. As hard as it was for him to admit, he'd been scared of taking a personal gamble that would leave him emotionally vulnerable. Then and there, he should have been brave enough to tell Natalie exactly how he felt about her, as Bobby had suggested. With the return of her memory, she needed to understand that his feelings for her were real, and not a part of some pretense designed to protect her.

Now that he had distance from the situation, it wasn't difficult for him to recognize that they were both running from a lifetime of tragic memories. They each harbored a fear of intimacy, feared trusting another person with their heart and soul. And yet he trusted Natalie with his life. He wanted her for keeps and forever, and he wasn't going to hide behind a painful past any longer when she was everything he'd ever dreamed of, and so much more. And that meant taking chances...like finally buying her the engagement ring she deserved. A symbol of his belief in her, and an eternal commitment to them as a couple. It was time he faced his own fears and took a risk with his emotions, and with Natalie.

He had nothing left to lose, except his heart.

NATALIE STOOD IN THE CENTER of her studio apartment Saturday morning, unable to believe that her entire life could be packed into only half a dozen boxes. That was the extent of the personal belongings she'd collected over the years. She still had a few breakable items she needed to wrap up, but other than that, she was nearly set to leave Oakland and start out fresh…yet again.

Her chest squeezed tight with heartache, a reaction she should have grown used to the past week without Noah, but one that only seemed to get worse with each day that passed. She hoped the distance of her move would help ease her misery. By Monday she would be gone, a memory to all who'd touched her life so briefly, yet so profoundly.

An overwhelming sadness washed over her, and she immediately chastised herself for wallowing in grief. She was used to being on her own, and she wasn't a stranger to starting over. Being raised in a multitude of foster homes had conditioned her to being resilient, and taught her not to get too attached to any one person or any particular place.

With the onslaught of her amnesia, all the rules she'd lived by for so long had been forgotten. She hadn't remembered that she needed to protect her emotions from Noah, which had allowed another part of her personality to develop and blossom. She'd been open and uninhibited with him, and her sense of freedom with Noah had felt so liberating. And while so many men through the years, Chad included, had treated her like a sex object with long legs and big breasts, she'd never once felt as though her body was the key factor in Noah's interest. He'd been noble until she'd seduced him, genuinely concerned about her safety, and so incredibly caring, sweet and tender.

He'd set her confined soul free, in a way she'd never imagined possible. In a way that began and ended with her love for Noah.

A shiver coursed through her, and she wrapped her arms around her stomach, realizing just how much she stood to lose. Despite their fabricated engagement, there was no doubt in her mind that Noah was a man to believe in and trust...with her heart and her future. Yet they both seemed to be running scared of all that had developed between them in such a short amount of time. Her desire to be with Noah was so overpowered by her fear of being too vulnerable and too dependent on another person that she wasn't facing what her heart truly wanted.

She straightened and lifted her chin mutinously. "It's time you stopped running, Natalie," she said to herself sternly, knowing that her instinct to flee had to end so she could finally take charge of her life, her future. And the only way she could accomplish that was to stay in Oakland and continue to make a life for herself here, as she'd always intended. She needed to follow her heart and embrace the challenge, instead of always taking the easy way out.

Chad was being prosecuted with numerous felony charges that would keep him behind bars for years. She had a job she enjoyed at Murphy's, and with just one more year of college, she'd have her social work degree.

Undoubtedly, she belonged *here,* in a way she'd never belonged anywhere else. And Noah, with his protective nature and caring ways, was the reason. And if she wanted a relationship with him to work, she had to be willing to meet him halfway, in all things—including love, respect and trust. *If* he was still interested in a relationship. After the way she'd walked out of his life last weekend, and hadn't contacted him since, she wasn't so sure.

A knock sounded at her door, startling her. Figuring it was the apartment manager delivering her check for half the amount of that month's rent, Natalie opened the door and found Noah standing on the other side of the threshold. She sucked in a startled breath, and her eyes widened in surprise.

"Noah!" she gasped, a surge of hope mingling with uncertainty.

A lazy smile eased up the corners of his mouth, as if he didn't have a care in the world, reminding her of the easygoing bachelor he'd been before he'd taken her into his protective custody as his "fiancée." While she felt like a disheveled mess in a pair of old cutoffs and an untucked blouse, he looked damned sexy and all male in a pair of casual pants and a blue shirt that stretched across the broad expanse of his chest. His dark hair was tousled, and his striking blue eyes appraised her in turn.

"Hello, Natalie," he drawled, his voice so deep

and sexy that her body surged with instantaneous awareness. "Can I come in?"

"Of course," she said, pasting on a semblance of a bright smile. He brushed past her into the small living area that encompassed her bed and a few necessary pieces of furniture.

Closing the door after him, she waved an apologetic hand at the open boxes scattered on the floor and the rumpled covers on her bed. "Sorry about the mess in here."

His gaze took in everything before coming back to rest on her, the flexing muscle in his jaw the only indication of emotion. "I heard you were leaving," he said gruffly.

She shoved her fingers into the back pockets of her shorts and affected a nonchalant attitude, though she craved his touch, his warmth. God, she'd missed him so much this past week! How had she believed that she could leave this man behind when he'd become her whole reason for living?

"I was thinking of moving to San Diego," she said.

He tipped his head curiously. "You were going to leave without saying goodbye?"

He looked and sounded genuinely hurt, and she hated that she was the source. She couldn't judge where they stood as a couple, or what the reason was for Noah's surprise visit, but with her decision to remain in Oakland firm, she needed to be honest and up front with him. "Noah…"

As if he didn't want to hear what she had to say,

he started toward her, completely, overwhelmingly male, making her words stall in her throat as he approached her so determinedly. Stopping inches away, he tangled his fingers into her hair and tipped her head back so she had no choice but to look up at him and meet his hot blue gaze.

"Well, here's a going-away present for you," he said, and covered her mouth with his own.

He kissed her greedily, selfishly, deeply, and she opened to him, taking whatever he was willing to give her. Their lips meshed, tongues mated, and he swallowed the moan that bubbled up from her throat. Just when she thought she'd go up in flames, he slowed the kiss, drawing out the lush sensations, branding her with the heat and taste of him, making her melt deep inside.

After what seemed like an eternity, he lifted his head, his expression both fierce and tender at the same time as he gauged her response to his parting gift.

Feeling thrown off balance, she pressed her hands against his chest to steady herself. "That certainly didn't feel like a goodbye kiss," she said, her voice husky with the desire he'd so easily stoked.

"You're right. It wasn't," he admitted, and feathered his thumb along her bottom lip in a soft caress. "It was a kiss asking you to take a chance on me, on *us*." He trailed his knuckles down her cheek, oh-so-gently. "All you have to do is say yes, Natalie," he murmured.

As much as she longed to surrender to his tempting overture, her cautious nature couldn't help but wonder if he was here out of some warped sense of obligation. Or were his actions motivated by guilt?

There was one way for her to find out. And if he gave her the answers she sought, she was all his in return.

"When you told me you loved me that last night we were together, did you mean it?" She held her breath as she waited for him to answer.

His gaze softened, glowing with the same emotion she'd seen in his eyes that night they'd bared their hearts to each other. "I *never* say anything I don't mean."

"Neither do I," she said, her meaning clear. "Not even when I'm under the influence of amnesia." She'd fallen in love with him then, and she still loved him now.

A slow, relieved smile spread across his gorgeous face. "*I love you,* Natalie," he said, the words resonating as strongly as the beat of her heart.

Tears of joy filled her eyes. "Oh, Noah, I love you, too," she whispered. And loving him gave her the strength to share her greatest fears. "And I've never been so afraid of wanting something as much as I want you."

"Then we have something in common, because all of this is brand new to me, too. I've never let myself need anyone before you, because I've lost too much in the past. Being a carefree bachelor was easier than risking rejection, in any form. But you... Ah, Natalie, you're worth every bit of that risk."

"So are you," she assured him. She may have

come to that conclusion only moments before he'd arrived, but she'd always known it in her heart. "After my parents died, I refused to form attachments to anything or anyone. Even with Chad, I might have lost myself in that relationship, but I never, ever risked anything emotional with him. I swear the very last thing I was looking for when I moved to Oakland was love. You made my pulse race every time our eyes met across the bar, but I fought my attraction to you for months, as you know."

"Yes, I do," he said, and chuckled.

She smiled, too, then grew serious again, wanting him to understand everything that led to her loving him. "But with the amnesia I lost so many inhibitions—nothing held back my emotion and desires for you. No matter the circumstances, no matter the pretense of our engagement, everything I felt for you was, and is, real and true."

He hugged her close and brushed his lips across her temple. His contented sigh sent warm breath rushing over her skin. "You don't know how happy I am to hear that."

She pulled back, just far enough to look into his eyes, needing that connection with him. "I also know if the accident never happened and I hadn't lost part of my memory, then we wouldn't be standing here like this, because I never would have allowed you close enough."

A dark brow lifted with amusement. "Are you suggesting that fate brought us together?"

"Maybe I am." She shrugged, and smiled up at

him. "Maybe we were meant to be together. I know I couldn't go back to the emptiness and solitude that was my life before you."

"Me, neither." He kissed her. Lightly. Tenderly. "Come home with me, Natalie, today. You're all packed and ready to go and my house is too damned big and lonely and quiet without you in it. You belong there with me."

"I love the way that sounds," she told him. "I've never truly belonged anywhere before."

"You're part of my life and family now," he said possessively. "So from now on, if you're going to run anywhere, run to *me*."

He was so calm, so steady and reliable. "I promise I will," she said, knowing he had shoulders broad enough to carry her burdens, and arms secure enough to keep her safe, forever and always.

But right now, at this very moment, she needed his body for an entirely different reason. Brazenly, she pushed him back, until his knees hit the edge of her bed and he fell back with a grunt of surprise. With him sprawled on the mattress, she crawled on top of him, straddling his thighs, welcoming the press of his erection against her feminine mound.

She sighed, and grinned down at Noah, having him finally right where she wanted him. "I hope you don't mind, but I have to have my way with you." She whipped off her blouse and bra, tossing them to the floor. "Right here. Right now." Skimming her hands beneath his shirt, she pulled it up and over his head, then bent to lave a nipple with her tongue, causing her heavy, aching breasts to graze his belly.

He thrashed and groaned, the muscles along his abdomen rippling. "Natalie...wait."

She wiggled out of her shorts and panties. "I've waited an entire week for you, and it's felt like a lifetime. I need you, Noah." She unbuckled the belt on his khaki pants, dipping her tongue into his navel, and lower, as she pulled the zipper down and released his rigid shaft for her to touch and caress.

She squeezed him in her fist, and he hissed out a breath, his hips bucking upward for a firmer stroke. "God, you're insatiable."

A slow, sinful smile curved her mouth as she tormented him with a soft, leisurely lap of her tongue along the swollen head of his penis. "You bring out the absolute best in me, including wanting you on a regular basis." She released him, only long enough to peel off his pants and briefs and drop the articles of clothing beside them on the bed. Then she was back on top of him, her body poised over his, his erection pressed against her slick opening. "Is that going to be a problem for you?"

Strangled laughter escaped him, and his glittering eyes met hers. "Hell, no. You've seen how my body reacts to just being near you."

"That's good to know." With her hands braced on his chest, she lowered herself onto him, taking him deep inside where she was hot and wet and silky soft, her expression reflecting supreme pleasure as she started to move rhythmically on him. "Because I don't think I'll ever get enough of you."

Noah understood the addiction, since he felt the same. But there was still one more thing he needed to do, *had* to do...just as soon as he took control of the situation. Pulling her down to his chest, he wrapped his arms around her and rolled her beneath him, so that he was in the dominant position.

She didn't seem to mind. She hooked her ankles against the back of his thighs and rocked him forward while she arched into him, causing him to slide impossibly deeper. Without a condom separating their flesh, the texture and friction of their bodies was more intense.

He grabbed her hip with one of his hands to still her provocative movements. "Natalie, *wait,*" he said through gritted teeth, feeling his own orgasm cresting and his restraint unraveling.

Startled, she blinked up at him, concern furrowing her brow. "Noah? What's wrong?"

He reached for his pants beside them, grateful they hadn't landed on the floor, and dug a small black velvet box out of the front pocket. Then he glanced back down at her, smiling gently at her wide eyes and uncertain expression.

He braced a forearm next to her head so he didn't crush her with his weight. "I had no idea how my visit here would end, but I was optimistic," he said.

"Is that..." She glanced from the small box to his face, disbelief and hope mingling in the depths of her gaze. "Oh, Noah, is that what I think it is?"

Lowering his head, he kissed her parted lips. "It's an engagement ring. I want to make you mine for real. No pretenses this time, Natalie." With his thumb, he flipped open the lid, revealing a gorgeous solitaire diamond ring that made her gasp. "I wanted this moment to be perfect, and do this right. You know, get down on one knee and ask you to marry me," he said wryly, knowing that this intimate moment would be one neither of them would ever forget, but that it wasn't a scenario they could easily share with friends and family.

Her soft hands framed his jawline, and her eyes shone with utter devotion and an abundance of love. "We're a part of each other, body and soul," she whispered, reminding him of that fact with a slight pull of her inner muscles around his shaft. "How much more perfect can a proposal get?"

A crooked grin lifted his mouth. "Say yes. Say that you'll marry me."

She didn't hesitate. "Yes, Noah Sommers, I'll marry you."

It took a bit of finagling, but he managed to remove the ring from the black velvet lining. Natalie held up her left hand, and he slipped the glittering diamond on her ring finger, making her his from that moment on.

Weaving their fingers together at the side of her head, he surged into her, strong and deep. "You do realize, don't you, that since I'm not wearing a condom that we might get an early start on that family we both want."

"Oh, let's hope," she said enthusiastically. "But if not, there's always tonight and tomorrow...."

He laughed and quieted her with a kiss, letting desire and passion take over, knowing fate would take care of everything else.